A King Production presents...

Bad Bitches Only ASSASSINS...

EPISODE 2

(Clout Chasers)

JOY DEJA KING

This novel is a work of fiction. Any references to real people, events, establishments, or locales are intended only to give the fiction a sense of reality and authenticity. Other names, characters, and incidents occurring in the work are either the product of the author's imagination or are used fictitiously, as those fictionalized events and incidents that involve real persons. Any character that happens to share the name of a person who is an acquaintance of the author, past or present, is purely coincidental and is in no way intended to be an actual account involving that person.

ISBN 10: 1-942217-36-6
ISBN 13: 978-1942217367
Cover concept by Joy Deja King
Cover model: Joy Deja King

Graphic design: www.anitaart79.wixsite.com/bookdesign
Typesetting: Anita J.

Library of Congress Cataloging-in-Publication Data;
A King Production
Assassins...Bad Bitches Only Episode 2/by Joy Deja King
For complete Library of Congress Copyright info visit;
www.joydejaking.com
Twitter @joydejaking

A King Production
P.O. Box 912, Collierville, TN 38027
A King Production and the above portrayal log are trademarks of A King Production LLC

This Book is Dedicated To My:

Family, Readers and Supporters.
I LOVE you guys so much. Please believe that!!

--Joy Deja King

Definition Of A Clout Chaser

/klout/ chas•er \ noun: A Person Who Strategically Associates Themselves With The Success Of A Popular Person To Gain Fame And Attention. This Personality Disorder Is Often Resembled As, "Riding The Wave" Without Concern For Damage Or Integrity.

A KING PRODUCTION
Bad Bitches Only
ASSASSINS...
EPISODE 2
(Clout Chasers)
JOY DEJA KING

Chapter One

WE RUN THIS

The striking Bentayga Speed pulled up to the exclusive mansion party, setting the tone for the night. The chauffeured driven limited edition black crystal finish Bentley truck, was punctuated by accents of bright St. James Red, dark tint lamps, radiator shell matrix with the laser like red lines splitting at the front, to encircle the lower bumper grilles. A fine line, painted entirely by hand, ran the length of the truck and door mirrors set off the exquisite vehicle. The 22" Speed wheels featured a gloss painted finish. Their uncompromising darkness complemented the body of the truck. Onlookers stood around in awe, waiting to see who was behind the closed door.

"You ready for this?" Shiffon asked Essence, lifting her body forward, off the diamond-quilted Alcantara seats.

Essence glanced out the tinted privacy glass and let out a deep sigh. "I guess."

"What you mean guess?" Shiffon raised an eyebrow, noticing how nervous her friend appeared to be.

"Girl, I don't know if I'm ready for this party." Essence shook her head. "It was cool when we were shopping around, having fun...preparing for it but now that we're here, I'm feeling a little intimidated," she admitted.

"You've been around money and mansions before," Shiffon frowned.

"Being around money from niggas who got hood fame, feels a lot different than mingling with famous celebrities making legit paper," Essence reasoned.

"See, that's where you fuckin' up. It ain't no different. Remember we used to attend those baller balls with Clay and Bezo. It would always be the same niggas. Some of them might switch up they girls, but it was a certain group of dudes gettin' paper, and they would all be at them type functions. That's how it is with these celebrity parties. They like regular mutha-fuckas cause they always seeing each other at the same shit," Shiffon explained.

"That's a good point." Essence stated.

"I know it is," Shiffon nodded. "It's a reason I made Alex come out his pocket and lease us this Bentley, have you wear that Dior dress, and me in this Cavalli. When we step out the truck, all eyes will be on us. Every clout chaser in there," she stressed, tilting her head in the direction of the mansion, "Is gonna think we run this. But the attitude has to match if we gon' pull this off. Do you follow me?"

"I do."

"I ain't hearing enough base in yo' voice." Shiffon wasn't convinced.

"Girl, I'm a female. I don't have base." Essence rolled her eyes.

"You better find it. You don't hear the base in my shit?!"

"But you've always had some tomboy in you."

"Well, you better get some tomboy in you too. We're assassins not trophy wives." Shiffon reminded Essence, in case she forgot they were there to do a job, and not find a man. "Remember, this our show... we run this!" She shouted at Essence in case she didn't hear her the first time.

Shiffon felt like she was a coach, preparing a boxer for a championship fight. She wanted to get Essence hyped up to win. Instead of feeling defeated before even stepping foot in the ring.

"I hear you. I'm ready...I'm ready!" Essence sounded as if she was trying to convince herself it was true. She grabbed an open bottle of champagne and poured herself one more glass. She tilted her head back, gulping it down in one take. "Let's do this!" She yelled, pumping herself up.

Shiffon knocked on the glass, letting the driver know to open the door for them. With the plunging, V-neck sleeveless nude colored jumpsuit, crystal studded five-inch stiletto heels and Ombre colored weave, Shiffon didn't need not one sip of courage juice. She was just mad there wasn't some theme music blasting when her open toe heel hit the pavement. As expected, the streets were staring hard as her and Essence strutted towards the main entrance. Anything less would've only been an insult to her.

"Damn, is this what Tupac meant when he said, *All Eyez On Me,* cause a bitch feeling in danger," Essence whispered to Shiffon, as they approached the door.

"That's the idea. If everybody out here talkin', that means the clout chasers watchin'," Shiffon winked, taking out the two gold chips each person had to present to security for entrance into the private party.

Essence barely had a moment to catch her breath walking into the marble foyer with a spectacular curved staircase and barrel ceiling. The first face she recognized was a delectable superstar NBA player. In the past, she'd fantasized sexing him a time or two while watching a game with Bezo, who was a basket_ball fanatic. Now here he was, standing within her reach like a forbidden piece of fruit.

"Don't you dare go over there," Shiffon warned. Knowing Essence was ready to come out her panties, and toss them at the tall, muscular, fine specimen.

"Excuse me?" Essence pretended to be clueless.

"Just keep walking." Shiffon nudged her, ready to drag Essence down the long hallway if need be.

"This party is so giving me *Less Than Zero* vibes but with a black cast," Essence remarked.

"*Less Than Zero*...why does that sound familiar to me?" Shiffon asked.

"Remember a few weeks ago, we woke up in the middle of the night and couldn't sleep, so we turned on the television and started watching that movie..."

"Oh yeah. That crazy movie with all those rich white kids in Beverly Hills doing coke." Shiffon's eyes widened. "I get the comparison," she nodded glancing around the large, opulent open space. *21 Savage* verse on *Rockstar* was even blaring out the speakers... *LA bitches, always asking where the coke at.*

But Shiffon and Essence weren't in LA, this was all going down in the Tuxedo Park area in Atlanta. An exclusive party to celebrate the multi-platinum success of an artist on Alex's, Fortune Five record label. And although there were sprinkles of coke users scattered throughout the house, premium weed was the preferred drug of choice.

"These people definitely know how to party," Essence observed, glancing around.

"But we're not here for that," Shiffon snapped, pulling on Essence's arm. "Come on…I see our mark."

"What's the rush? Nobody tryna leave this party," Essence remarked, steady gazing around the room. "Our mark ain't going nowhere." She was enjoying her celebrity watching a bit too much for Shiffon's taste.

"I'm not interested in who's leaving the party. I'm waiting for an arrival." Shiffon eyed her watch, before taking a seat on the L shape midcentury style velvet couch, in the corner.

"They have this area set up real cute and everything but why are we sitting in this vivinity?" Essence sulked. "I mean ain't nobody over here."

"That's all about to change. Now sit down and follow my lead."

"Can I get you ladies something to drink?" one of the servers came up to them and asked.

"I'll have a glass of champagne." Essence requested.

"Cancel the champagne!" Shiffon quickly said. "We'll have two bottle waters." She smiled politely, letting the server know he could go.

"What the fuck?!"

"You already had enough champagne when we were in the truck." Shiffon cut her eyes at Essence.

"What part aren't you understanding. We're working tonight. I need your mind right. You'll be no use to me drunk."

"There you go looking at that damn watch again," Essence rolled her eyes.

"And right on time, here comes our guy," Shiffon nodded, crossing her legs.

A few seconds later the music switched from a Drake record, to the current #1 song on the Billboard charts, by a new artist named Enzo. Who the record label, Fortune Five was hosting this elaborate party for. The music industry elite had anointed him as the man who would bring R&B back. And with him having the number one song and album, he was proving them right.

"Girl," Essence tapped Shiffon's hand. " You didn't tell me this party was for Enzo. That nigga is so fine," she gasped. Staring as he and his entourage walked towards them.

"Please close your mouth," Shiffon said, when Enzo and his crew filled up the sitting area directly across from them. "Don't you see he has a date," she cracked with a half-smile.

"Who cares...she's pretty though...I. guess." Essence hated to admit.

"She is a beauty but so are you. No need to be jealous," Shiffon winked.

Essence's competitive nature had her totally immersed in the mirror, touching up her makeup. Double checking to ensure her face was flawless. She was too busy analyzing her appearance to even notice Shiffon was closely monitoring a group of women standing several feet away. Her eyes then shifted to Enzo and his lady friend who had their full fledge make out session on display.

"Them muthafuckas need to get a room," Essence scoffed.

"Don't be mad Enzo is tonguing her down and not you," Shiffon teased, enjoying the fourplay between the sexy couple. But she was about to enjoy the fireworks even more.

Interesting...Martina is steady arguing with her homegirls but keeping her distance from the person she really wants to dig her claws into. I wonder how long she'll be able to keep her cool before that hot temper of hers takes over, Shiffon thought to herself. *Lemme give her the push she needs...*

"Could you tell the photographer to come over here please," Shiffon told the server.

"Of course," he smiled.

"I thought you said we were working?"

"We are."

"Then why are you having the photographer come over and take our picture? I mean I don't mind, cause I look damn good tonight but I'm just surprised," Essence shrugged.

"Oh, the photographer ain't for us." Shiffon shook her head.

"If not us, then who?" Essence wanted to know.

"Them." Shiffon pointed her ballerina nail towards Enzo. The photographer didn't need much incentive to start clicking away. With mostly everyone at his table being drunk or high, no one was paying much attention to the man with the camera. No one except for Martina, who was feeling extremely left out. It was already driving her crazy another female was making out with Enzo at a party, but the possibility of pics being spread all across the blogs and social media was her breaking point.

Essence turned in the direction Shiffon was pointing. "I see Enzo and his bimbo...I mean date still suckin' faces. Why you tryna give that chick free press. I'm sure she'd love to see photos of her and Enzo kissing all over the internet."

"Maybe but I'm sure someone else will be sick to her stomach." Shiffon had a mischievous grin on her face, staring back at the small group of women who appeared to be arguing amongst each other. They were pulling Martina's arm as if trying to hold her back but she broke loose.

"Damn, that chick look pissed. Homegirl betta slow down, before she break the heel on those bad ass shoes she wearing and fall the fuck down," Essence laughed.

"Listen, I need you to go over there," Shiffon whispered to Essence. "And keep those ladies busy."

"Over there where them chicks yappin'...why?!"

"Because I don't need any interference. Remember, keep them entertained and out my way." Shiffon hurried off but then slowed down when she got near Enzo's table. She stood within ear distance while Martina tried to go Brooklyn Finest on Enzo and his date.

"Enzo, what happened to you comin' to this party solo. I thought it was all business for you tonight!" Martina popped.

"Yo, you supposed to be in NYC. What you doin' in the A?" Enzo spoke smoothly, with his hand placed on his date's inner thigh and her leg draped across his lap.

"I came here to surprise you. I figured you be happy to see me since we was just in LA together. But you wit' the next bitch!" Martina spit.

"Slow down, Ma." Enzo put his hand up. "Don't do that here. This a celebration." Enzo tilted down his sunglasses making eye contact with Martina.

"Baby, don't let her ruin our party." Enzo's date whispered, licking her tongue across his earlobe.

"I got this," Enzo replied, with no worries detected in his voice.

"You got this...really nigga?! Is that how you gon' play me?" Martina's fiery temper was on the verge of erupting.

"Enzo, put a leash on this bitch before I have to dog walk her." His date stated, leaning in to give him another kiss.

The shade sent Martina nuclear. Before anyone

could stop her, she had her hands around the woman's throat. Doing her best to choke her out. But she'd sorely underestimated the leggy beauty. Enzo's date, didn't do any scratching or pulling. She balled up her fist and pounded it on the side of Martina's head.

"Ouch!" Martina screamed out but the girl wasn't done. She flipped Martina down on her back. Jumped on top of her and began delivering an onslaught of punches.

"I think that's enough." Shiffon muttered under her breath before yanking the girl by her hair, and dragging her off a bloody Martina. "You need to leave her tha fuck alone!" She gave the chick a back handed smack, causing her to tumble back into Enzo.

"Damn you a'ight?" he asked.

"Nah! I'm 'bout to fuck her up!" The chick tried to stand back up but her balance was off.

"Bring it! I'm standing right here." Shiffon taunted the woman. Postured in a fighting stance.

The woman rose up as if she was about to charge at Shiffon but Enzo held her back. "Leave it alone." He insisted.

"You better listen to yo' man, or you gon' be the one gettin' dog walked," Shiffon warned.

"Man, where the fuck is security?" Enzo scoffed. But everyone in his entourage was so lit, they were either still joking about the girl fight that just transpired, or too out of it to care about finding security."

"Don't worry about security, we leaving," Shiffon

smacked, grabbing some napkins off the table. "How you feeling, are you okay?" she kneeled down and asked Martina, who was still on the floor. Enzo's date had got the best of her but Shiffon thought Martina was still on the floor, not because she couldn't get up but because she was embarrassed.

"I'm fine. I can't believe Enzo let that girl do me like this," Martina complained.

"Here, wipe the side of your mouth." Shiffon said, handing Martina a napkin.

"Thank you and I appreciate you lookin' out for me. You don't even know me. You ain't have to do that shit," Martina said, dabbing the blood off her mouth.

"I felt bad for you. You too pretty to get yo' face all fucked up." Shiffon knew chicks like Martina loved to be told how cute they are.

"Do I look really bad?" Martina questioned, feeling self-conscious.

"No. I got her off of you before that happened. You still gorgeous as ever." Shiffon was saying all the right things.

"You really looked out," Martina smiled.

"Come on, let me get you outta here. People are beginning to circle." Shiffon helped Martina up. She immediately tried to fix her hair and clothes as much as possible, before walking back over towards Enzo's table.

Damn, this broad ain't about to start tryna fight again. If she don't leave this shit alone, Shiffon thought to herself staying close behind Martina.

"That's fucked up how you played me, Enzo. But I got something for you...watch! So fuck you and yo' bitch!" Martina fussed, before turning to walk away.

"Girl, don't worry about him. He's not worth the energy," Shiffon stressed to her.

"Nah, that nigga ain't gonna get away wit' treating me like this," Martina continued to fuss. "And where the fuck is my friends!" She shouted looking around. "Look at them! They over there talkin' to some niggas." Martina stormed off and Shiffon trailed behind her.

Shiffon had already spotted Martina's crew because Essence was with them, all up in that basketball player's face. She didn't want to be the one to notice them first, so she kept quiet. By the time Shiffon walked up, Martina was in the midst of cursing them out.

"Ya'll supposed to have my back. You see my face! If it wasn't for this chick..." Martina scanned her surroundings searching for Shiffon. "There you go," she said pulling her closer. "Damn, you looked out for me and I don't even know yo' name."

"It's Desi."

"You see this Desi chick!" Martina's body language and voice were extra animated. "I just met her tonight and she fought for me. Shut that hoe down! Ya'll my friends but over here talkin' to some niggas while a bitch beatin' my ass!" She yelled.

While Martina continued shouting at her friends and they pleaded their case, Shiffon pulled Essence over to the side. "You just had to find an excuse to talk to that NBA player didn't you."

"I kept them broads out yo' business, right. So what's the problem?"

"Essence, when we working, niggas supposed to be the last thing on yo' mind, unless they the target. Dick will always be available."

"I can't tell." Essence folded her arms, annoyed. "Because a bitch ain't had no dick in forever."

"Fine. You wanna fuck. Go fuck that nigga then." Shiffon put her hand out as if saying get the hell on then.

"Don't be like that, Shiffon."

"You mean Desi. Cause like I said, we working, at least I am. If you ain't tryna work, then by all means go fuck that nigga or whatever dick you can find and jump on top of."

Essence let out a deep sigh. "You done made yo' point. I get it. When we working, all that other shit is a non-factor. I can fuck on my own time."

"Exactly." Shiffon said, turning around when she heard Martina calling her.

"Desi!" Martina came walking over to them. "We're about to go get something to eat. Come with us. Of course I'm treating. Anything for the bitch that had my back." Martina hugged Shiffon.

"Thanks girlie. Let's go," she smiled. And just like that, Shiffon had bonded with the Queen B herself, and by doing so, infiltrated the scandalous clout chasers.

Chapter Two

NO NEW MEMBERS

"Fuck, them chicks can party," Shiffon moaned, opening the refrigerator to get some juice. "Martina got knocked on her ass and that shit didn't slow her down not one bit. I thought we was gonna stay out until the sun came up."

"Shit, we would've, if her friend Tish didn't get a call from that nigga, and had to get back to the hotel," Essence reminded Shiffon.

"True. I ain't neva been so happy for a bitch to have some dick waiting on her. Them broads got my ass feeling old. Like did we party that hard when we were they age?" Shiffon questioned.

"Bitch, you act like we senior citizens. They like what anywhere from twenty to twenty-two. We only twenty-five," Essence frowned.

"Then why the fuck am I still so damn tired and it's the middle of the afternoon?" Shiffon wondered.

"Probably because before Clay had to sit down and do his bid, he had you on lockdown. If you wasn't with him, then you was in the crib. You ain't ran the streets in years. Give it some time, your body will adjust."

"Fuck that. I need to figure out which one of those chicks is the FBI informant, kill they ass and get the fuck on. Them hoes is gon' wear me out," Shiffon complained, hearing the doorbell.

"You expecting somebody?" Essence asked.

"Damn, I forgot it was two already." Shiffon looked at the clock on the microwave. "Yeah, that's Leila," she said, heading out the kitchen to get the door.

"Leila...who the fuck is that?" Essence was curious to know, right behind Shiffon.

"Is it two in the afternoon or two in the morning," Leila cracked, when Shiffon let her in. "You look like you just rolled out of bed."

"Pretty much," Shiffon said closing the door. "Leila this is Essence."

"Hey! Nice to meet you. I've heard a lot about you," Leila smiled widely.

"Really? I ain't heard not nothing about you." Essence glanced over at Shiffon, waiting for some background info on this chick she'd never met before.

"This townhouse is beautiful. Shiffon, you live here by yourself?" Leila questioned, not even acknowledging what Essence said.

"No, Three of us live here. Me, Essence and my cousin Bailey. She's not here right now though."

"It's definitely big enough for three people. It looks super expensive too," Leila reasoned, glancing around at all the upgrades.

"Having three incomes most definitely helps," Shiffon acknowledged.

"Shoot, is there space for a fourth roommate," Leila laughed.

"No. It's only three bedroom, three bath." Essence made sure to jump in the conversation and push the idea of a fourth roommate right out of Leila's mind.

"Oh." Leila sounded disappointed but not discouraged.

"I know we just met but you look mad familiar to me. You sure we ain't been around each other before?" Essence pressed. Thinking maybe she was some random chick she'd caught her ex Bezo fucking with.

"Nope, we've definitely never met before," Leila said without hesitation.

"You sound awfully sure?" Essence smacked.

"Because I am. I'm from Vegas. This is my first time in Atlanta."

"Essence, the reason Leila looks so familiar to you, is because she was Enzo's date at the party last night," Shiffon explained.

"That was you!" Essence shouted.

Leila and Shiffon both paused and stared at Essence for a minute.

"Damn, you sound mad." Leila laughed.

"So that entire fight between you, Martina and this chick," Essence said, pointing at Leila with an attitude, "Was all one big farce?"

"Pretty much. I mean, I didn't expect for Leila to stomp on Martina's ass like that though," Shiffon giggled.

"Originally that wasn't my plan but when she tried to choke the life outta me, I got pissed."

"What did you expect when you hit her wit' that Cardi B dog walk shade." Shiffon and Leila both burst out laughing.

"You gotta admit that was a nice touch," Leila boasted. "If that jab didn't make her ready to fight, then nothing would. But shiiit, I didn't expect for you to backhand smack me like that neither," Leila started laughing again.

"I promised I wouldn't leave no marks and I

didn't...right?" Shiffon stated.

"You did keep your promise." Leila gave Shiffon a pound like they went way back. "Plus, the extra oomph you put in yo' slap, made the entire altercation appear real."

"Yep, it fuckin' did, cause I damn sure was fooled! Shiffon, how could you keep me out the loop? I thought Bad Bitches Only was a partnership and we was in this together. You keeping me in the dark, don't sound like no partnership to me!" Essence's accusatory tone, made all the giggling and laughing stop immediately.

"I planned on telling you today but I overslept and lost track of time. Then Leila showed up before I had a chance to break everything down."

"I should've been a part of the planning process. Why all the secrecy and why did you pick her to be locking lips wit' Enzo?" Essence was rambling off questions.

"Picked me as opposed to who...you?" Leila groaned. "For yo' information, Shiffon didn't pick me for Enzo. I had already been dealing wit' him."

"Essence, maybe I should've told you about the game plan but I figured the less you knew the better. I wasn't even sure how this shit was gon' play out."

"Yeah, this was like a test run for me. Shiffon was being cautious by not telling you," Leila said to Essence, defending Shiffon's decision. "But if I do say so myself, I think I proved last night, I would be an asset to the Bad Bitches Only crew," she winked.

"I agree," Shiffon nodded.

"Hold tha fuck up!" Essence stepped in between the two women. "Are you saying, this chick is gonna be a part of Bad Bitches Only?"

"What's yo' problem wit' me?" Leila wanted to know. "Is it Enzo...did you used to fuck wit' the nigga... do you still fuck wit' the nigga? If so, it's all good. Me and him ain't on no exclusive shit."

"Everybody chill for a second." Shiffon put her head down, thinking she hadn't gotten enough sleep last night to deal with this shit. "Essence, I told you we would be adding new females to the crew. It was just a matter of finding the right chicks."

"What makes you think she's the right chick?" Essence was obviously not convinced.

"Did you..." Leila jumped in, ready to oppose every objection Essence had.

"I got this." Shiffon put her hand up, cutting Leila off. "Initially, I wasn't even tryna recruit new members for Bad Bitches Only. I came across Leila by accident, while researching Martina and her friends. I had to figure out how to get into they inner circle because from following their social media pages, I knew it wasn't gonna be easy. They're a pretty tight clique."

"What does any of that have to do wit' you bringing this bootleg Naomi Campbell into the fold?"

"Did you just call me..." Leila was ready to curse Essence out.

"Leila, please sit down and be quiet. Let me handle this!" Shiffon cut her off again, losing her patience with both of them. "Getting back to what I was saying. Martina basically lives her entire life via social media. Through that, I realized she was seeing Enzo. I then started monitoring Enzo's social media, and although he loves the ladies, I came across a few women he seemed to keep in rotation, one being Leila. I reached out to five of them, three I met with in person. Out of the three women, Leila seemed like she would know how to get the biggest rise out of Martina. It wasn't until we started plotting on how this would go down, did I start considering her for Bad Bitches Only."

"And I delivered!" Leila shouted from the couch.

"Yeah you did," Shiffon turned to Leila and said. "I had my doubts you would but they were all erased last night. Leila played her part with perfection, from beginning to end. She'll be an asset."

"Don't I have a say on who should be a part of this crew?" Essence wasn't letting this go.

"Bad Bitches Only was my idea. Besides me, yeah you were the first member but that doesn't mean you get to dictate who I decide to bring on. Of course I want your input but not when it's based on something like jealousy," Shiffon scoffed.

"I'm not jealous of her!" Essence shot back.

"Then why are you being so fuckin' petty? Leila delivered what I needed last night. Martina is all up my ass. This time yesterday, she had no clue who the fuck I was. That's a lot of fuckin' progress in less than twenty-four hours. Leila played a major role in making the shit happen. So you will deal or..."

"Or what?" now it was Essence who was cutting folks off mid-sentence. "You gon' kick me out the group, like I'm an unwanted member of Destiny's Child. Bitch, you ain't Beyonce."

"Of Bad Bitches Only...yes the fuck I am. You seem to keep forgetting I'm running a business, Essence. You wanna make this about our friendship but I strongly advise you figure out how to separate the two."

"You know what, Shiffon. Fuck you and Bad Bitches Only!" Essence fumed, storming out the room.

Chapter Three

STUNTS

Martina was in her hotel room, staring at her reflection in the bathroom mirror. Because she used her hands to block her face, there was only a slight bruise on her cheek from the onslaught of punches she received from Leila last night. But that didn't stop Martina from being pissed. The more she thought about it, the angrier she became.

That nigga Enzo ain't even called, sent a text or nothing making sure I'm straight. Less than a week ago I was laid up wit' him for three days straight. Fuckin', suckin', poppin' pills and everything else. Then he let the next hoe jump on me and he don't even blink. I see you Enzo and now you 'bout to see me too, Martina seethed stomping out the bathroom in a rage.

"Where my phone at?" Martina asked Kayla and Flora who were sitting in the living room area watching television.

"Last time I saw you with it, was when we were outside on the balcony," Kayla told her.

"That's right." Martina went outside to the balcony and retrieved her phone. She then picked up her makeup bag off the table and headed back to the bathroom.

"You 'bout to get dressed...we going somewhere?" Flora called out.

"Not yet. I have something else I need to get done first," Martina shouted back before slamming the bathroom door close.

"Enzo must've not hit her up yet," Kayla shrugged, getting back to eating the food that was just delivered from room service.

"That nigga make her so moody. He cute and all but maybe she need to leave Enzo alone. He ain't worth the stress," Flora reasoned.

"To Martina he is. Since she started fuckin' wit' him and posting pics when they together, she done got over two hundred thousand more followers on Instagram and their pics get mad likes. It's for sure raised her profile," Kayla nodded.

"When you put it like that, I guess you right," Flora agreed.

In between eating their food and watching television, the women continued gossiping about Martina, Enzo and any other dude in the industry on their radar. They were enjoying themselves but the kee-keeing came to a halt when Martina entered the sitting area with a black eye.

"What tha fuck happened to your face?!" Kayla put her food down and stood up.

"Not shit," Flora mumbled, continuing to watch tv.

"I'ma need you to turn that shit off. I'm about to go live on Instagram and don't need no background noise," Martina said, checking her reflection in the mirror one last time. All she had on was a hotel bathrobe when she turned the camera on herself and went live.

"What is she doing?" Kayla turned to Flora and asked, looking baffled.

"Not sure but I'm guessing Martina 'bout to pull one of her stunts," Flora shrugged. Unlike Kayla, Flora had known Martina for years. They both grew up in one of the five boroughs in New York City. The women connected when they were teenagers, while attending the same school of the arts in Manhattan. They soon became inseparable. Not due to their love of the arts but their thirst for fame.

What up everybody! You know I always keep it one hundred wit' ya. So I had to jump on here right quick and show you this black eye I received courtesy of Enzo. Ya know I been fuckin' wit' that nigga for a minute. I got mad pics posted all over my page wit' him but all that shit coming down after this video. Last night he had a party here in Atlanta to celebrate his number one song and album. I wanted to surprise my boo and showed up. The surprise was on me. That nigga was wit' another Bitch and he showed his ass cause I busted him. I'm done wit' that nigga! Fuck Enzo! Martina ended her rant with those closing words and signed off.

"Yo, you fuckin' crazy!" Kayla gasped.

"You call it crazy, I call it brilliant." Martina smiled widely, showcasing every tooth in her mouth. "Watch all the new followers I'm gonna get. Shit, I'll probably be the #1 trending topic," she bragged.

"But you lied on that nigga!" Kayla protested.

"They don't know that shit and by the time anyone finds out, my name will be bubbling all through social media. In the meantime, let the dragging begin on Enzo's ass," Martina beamed, scrolling through the comments on his Instagram page.

"Man, you need to post a video right now saying you was just playin'!" Kayla insisted. "Flora, say something!"

"Girl, you getting yourself all worked up for nothing. This the type of silly shit Martina do. No sense in tryna change her mind," Flora scoffed.

"Fuck Enzo! He deserved that shit!" Martina fussed, taking a few selfies of what her friends believed to be a self-inflicted black eye.

"I know you pissed at Enzo but fuckin' up yo' face just so you could trash him on Instagram is too much." Kayla shook her head.

"I ain't that crazy. Not fuckin' up my pretty face for that nigga," Martina giggled, disappearing into the bathroom but quickly reappearing with a wet towel. "It's just makeup," she laughed wiping off her face. "That's why I took pics, so I can upload the proof before going back to my fabulous self," she winked continuing to wipe away any trace of a fake blackeye.

"I told you Martina was a stunt puller," Flora reminded Kayla.

"Oh...and look who finally decided to call me." Martina held up her iPhone. "Bad news really does travel fast," she smirked, declining Enzo's incoming call.

Chapter Four

COMPLICATIONS

Shiffon was in her car driving, on her way to meet Martina for lunch, when she noticed Alex was calling. "I wonder what he wants. It's a bit too soon for an update," Shiffon said out loud before answering his call. "Hey Alex, what can I do for you?"

"I need to see you."

"Okay, ummm what about later on this evening or

tomorrow afternoon?"

"I need to see you now."

With the deliberate tone in Alex's voice and the amount of money he was paying her for the job, Shiffon had no intentions of objecting to his request. Her lunch date with Martina would have to wait, as her client came first.

"I'm on the way." Shiffon ended her call with Alex and grabbed another phone, first making sure it was the one designated for her alias Desi. Due to her new profession, Shiffon now had multiple cells. She sent Martina a text letting her know she couldn't make it for lunch but if she was available they could do dinner. After handling that, Shiffon headed to Alex's place.

She arrived at the sophisticated residence above the prestigious St. Regis Hotel, within fifteen minutes. This was her third time coming to Alex's condo, and she was left mesmerized with each visit. From the custom millwork, hardwood and inlaid marble floors, painted ceilings, incredible kitchen by Design Galleria and breathtaking views of the southern skyline would leave even the most disparaging guest in awe.

"Come in," Alex said, as Shiffon followed him to the living room which was off the gallery and dining room. "Have a seat."

"What did you need to see me about?" Shiffon wanted to know. Alex's demeanor was always more so on the icy side but Shiffon couldn't help but notice it was even chillier than usual.

"I gave you a substantial budget, so you could attend Enzo's party. Money you promised would be well spent."

"And it was."'

"How?"

"We haven't spoken since the party. I was waiting to update you once I gathered more information but I've made a meaningful connection with the ringleader of that clique. Which means I'm closer to finding out which one of them is an informant for the FBI. I call that a success."

"When you say the ringleader, I'm assuming you're speaking of Martina," Alex said, putting his glass of cognac down and leaning back in his chair.

"Of course," Shiffon nodded.

"When was the last time you spoke to her?"

"I was actually on my way to meet Martina for lunch when you called. I had to come meet with you, so now we're having dinner tonight."

"I see."

"I thought you would sound more pleased," Shiffon commented, bothered by the grimace expression on Alex's face.

"You told me you were keeping tabs on the women including their social media presence."

"I am."

"Then how in the fuck didn't you see that fame-whore Martina go live on Instagram lying on my artist? You didn't get a notification?" Alex barked.

"I guess I didn't." Shiffon hated to be caught off guard by some bullshit shenanigans Martina pulled but kept her confident composure.

"Then you need to turn that shit on. You should know they every move, including when they shit, with the amount of money I'm paying you," Alex fumed, now standing up.

Shiffon had never seen Alex lose his cool but the nigga was vexed. She was afraid to ask what went down when Martina decided to go live but knew she had to.

"You're absolutely right. It will never happen again. What exactly did Martina say when she went live?"

"She had a blackeye and claimed Enzo gave it to her at his party because she caught him with another woman. Do you know how damaging that shit is. I have several endorsement deals lined up for Enzo and that shit might be in serious jeopardy."

Alex was holding his glass so tightly, Shiffon was concerned it was going to break in his hand. But she understood his frustration. Martina didn't fight fair. Shiffon underestimated how grimy the clout chaser could be.

"There were plenty of witnesses at Enzo's party, including me. I'm sure they can all attest he never laid a hand on Martina." Shiffon was doing her best to minimize the damage she probably caused.

"That shit don't matter." Alex shook his head. "It's about perception. The media starts drooling at the mouth when they can run with a story about a young black man, with fame and money being a woman beater. They'll spin this bullshit for the next three months. I'm tempted to have you kill that bitch right now, regardless if she's the informant or not."

"Alex, I have to advise you against that. With the negativity surrounding her connection with Enzo right now, it'll make him the prime suspect," Shiffon reasoned.

"I said I was tempted, not that I want you to do it. I know what's at stake. My record label is under enough scrutiny. First Taz Boy and now Enzo. These chicks are a problem."

"Listen, let me work on fixing this situation with Martina."

"Fix it how?"

"Do some damage control with this lie she's put out there about Enzo. I have an idea," Shiffon told him. "I'll need your cooperation but at least we can kill the buzz before it gets any louder."

"Do what you have to do. You have my full cooperation. But while you fixing this bullshit with Martina, I need you to find that informant. I can't stand a snake, especially when they're in my own backyard," Alex stressed.

"Point taken. I'll be in touch."

Shiffon left Alex's condo with a headache. When

he hired Bad Bitches Only to pinpoint who the FBI informant was, she assumed the hardest part would be finding a way to infiltrate the ladies crew. But with this new info Alex dropped on her, Shiffon realized this job would be much more complicated than she anticipated.

Chapter Five

GET MONEY

Enzo was a tall, slender nigga with a long thick dick to match. Besides belting out love ballads and being a beast on the piano, he had one other passion...pussy. Not only did he love getting lost in the warmth of a woman's insides, he also enjoyed their company. Some he liked more than others and Leila was one of his favorites.

"Yes Daddy!" Leila called out as Enzo pulled her hair while hitting it from the back. She bit down on her bottom lip as his strokes became more intense.

"Don't you love this dick?" Enzo moaned, watching the shape of Leila's ass bounce back and forth on his rock hard tool.

"Yes Daddy!" She called out again but this time even louder and with more desire in her voice. This only aroused Enzo further. He wanted to go deeper until he could reach her ribs.

Leila could feel his dick throbbing and her pussy kept getting wetter as Enzo's grip became tighter. "Baby, I'm 'bout to cum," she wailed, biting down on the pillow. She wasn't sure how much more she could take. Leila wanted Enzo to get his before reaching her orgasm but his stamina was ridiculous. Handling a dude with a big dick and endurance was a chore. Leila wasn't sure she was up for the task today but she kept putting in work until she heard Enzo groan, then collapse after he finally was able to cum.

Leila's ability to keep up with Enzo's insatiable sex drive, was the main reason she was one of his favorites. And unlike many of his other sexual partners, she didn't need to use illicit drugs to do so. Leila was the cardio queen, so to her having sex with Enzo was equivalent to the ultimate workout at the gym.

"Damn, I needed that," Enzo grunted, leaning over kissing Leila on the back of her neck. "The stress is real right now."

"Babe, don't worry about that lyin' ass broad. Nobody believe that shit." Leila turned to Enzo and said, knowing exactly who had him feeling under pressure.

"Tell that shit to all them muthafuckas who keep flooding my social media pages."

"Ignore those trolls."

"If only shit was that easy."

"I don't understand why you won't let me put the truth out there. That it was me who stumped Martina's silly ass and not you."

"My management team think that's the wrong move. They released a statement saying it ain't true and now they waitin' for the shit to die down. Until then, I'ma keep a low profile."

Fuck! Never did I think teaming up with Shiffon to create an opening for her to befriend Martina, would bring all this chaos to Enzo's life. He doesn't deserve the backlash he's getting behind this girl's bullshit. Man oh man, that chick is a piece of work. If I had the slightest clue, she'd cause this much trouble, I would've dragged her ass all through the party instead of just laying her out on the floor, Leila thought to herself as she stared up at the ceiling fan filled with guilt.

"You up to letting me relieve some more stress?" Enzo leaned up in the bed and asked Leila.

"I'm game," Leila lied and said. Taking all those inches actually left her exhausted and her body somewhat sore. But since she felt partially responsible for the chaos he was dealing with, Leila felt obligated to give Enzo some sympathy pussy.

"There's my shero!" Martina ran over to Shiffon and gave her a hug when she entered the restaurant. "You look cute too! Bitch, who bought you those Louboutin's?! They're to fuckin' die for." Martina was hyperventilating over the sparkling crystal ladder straps Raynibo Cage sandal, with rainbow hues and lifted by a tapered stiletto heel.

"They were gift," Shiffon said coyly. Following behind Martina and the hostess, who led them to their table. She knew the pricey shoes would have Martina foaming at the mouth. It was the only reason she dug into Alex's generous expense budget to buy them.

"Bitch, I need a friend like yours." Martina smacked. "Is this the same friend that hooked you up wit' that sick Bentley truck?"

"How did you know about the Bentley truck?" Shiffon questioned, placing the tip of her nail on the menu, pretending to be surprised.

"I make it my business to know everything, especially when it comes to bad bitches new on the scene," Martina smiled. "But if you must know, it was my girl Tish. She was outside talking to some dude, when she saw you and your homegirl step out the truck. When she realized you were the chick that was ready to brawl for me, she was impressed."

"Nothing to be impressed about." Shiffon kept her attitude very nonchalant.

"Yes the fuck it is? You see my own clique was nowhere to be found when that girl with Enzo tried to jump on me." Martina frowned up her face, glancing through the menu.

There was no tried to it, Martina. Leila pounded on that ass. All I did was stop her from finishing you off. But go head and spin that tale, girl, Shiffon laughed to herself.

"Speaking of Enzo, I could've sworn I read somewhere that people are saying he beat you up or some shit?"

"Oh, you heard about that shit?!" Martina laughed loudly, causing people in the restaurant to turn in their direction. "Girl, I was on Instagram live, wit' my face all fucked up. Damn, I wish that shit stayed up so I can show you. I even posted a selfie lookin' like I had a black eye. Muthafuckas was draggin' that nigga too!" She continued to joke.

Shiffon sat back amazed at how Martina didn't give two fucks about trying to ruin Enzo's reputation. She was giggling, laughing and cracking jokes, like she'd participated in a harmless prank. *This heffa is dangerous.* "So wait, you're the one that started that rumor?" Shiffon played it like she was clueless.

"Yeah..." Martina gave Shiffon a, you can't be that

dumb look, while giving the waitress their drink order. "Of course I started the rumor. That's what his ass get for fuckin' me over wit' that raggedy bitch he was with. He should've known better not to cross me. I don't play that shit."

"I feel you but I think you might be playing this one wrong."

"Excuse me?!" It was obvious Martina wasn't used to anybody questioning her decisions, based on the how dare you glare on her face.

"I mean trashing Enzo on social media will bring some traffic to your page, likes and temporary buzz but wouldn't you prefer something more substantial?"

Martina's eyes lit up. Shiffon could tell she was speaking her language. "Substantial how?"

"Maybe some financial compensation if you'll retract your original statement. I mean at the very least, that nigga can hit you off wit' some money, for tryna let that girl embarrass you in public."

"You know what...you right! That nigga do need to hit me off wit' some paper. But Enzo so pissed at me, he ain't gon' give me shit. And it's not like I can threaten to have him locked up. I would need to file a police report. And since he didn't lay no hands on me, and he got witnesses to attest to it, I would end up fuckin' myself up," Martina fussed.

"True but in the social media world, you don't need no receipts for people to believe whatever story you selling. So his clean cut image is taking a major hit.

Maybe Enzo don't want to come off no paper but I'm sure his record label would love to kill this story."

"Desi, girl you might be on to something," Martina nodded. "The thing is, the nigga who owns the record label Enzo's on. I don't know how to get at him, plus I heard he's an asshole."

"You in luck. My cousin's bestie fuck wit' him," Shiffon lied.

"Yo, you know a chick who fuck wit' Alex?! That nigga so rich. Is he stingy or do he be coming off that paper?" Martina was ready to hit Shiffon with a million questions. "I don't know not one bitch he fuck wit'. I thought the nigga was gay. How the girl look...she cute?"

"She's stunning," Shiffon smiled, knowing that would get under Martina's skin.

"Forreal...she look better than you?"

"It depends what you like...your type," Shiffon shrugged. "I will say she's very lowkey. Not the on the scene type."

"Oh you mean boring." Martina quickly dismissed whoever the chick might be. Playing with her dimensional honey blonde A-Line bob, with a deep angular part and side swept bang. "Do you think you can use her to get to Alex?" was all she wanted to know.

"For sure."

"Cool. Make it happen. I heard he got a female clothing line too. Throw in a sponsored post on Instagram with me modeling some of the clothes. Of course

I get to keep all the outfits I pick out," Martina added.

"Of course. I'll get on it," Shiffon beamed.

"Girl, fuck them other broads I be with. Brains, beauty, fashion game on point annnnd connections. You got everything I need in a new best friend!" Martina had no shame, holding up her wine, so the women could click glasses. "Cheers!"

"Yes cheers...to gettin' that money!" Shiffon played up her eagerness to assist with the money shakedown. This only drew Martina in more. All she saw was dollar signs.

Chapter Six

WELCOME TO THE FOLD

"So what you tryna do, sneak in and sneak out?" Bailey walked in Essence's bedroom and asked as she was packing her clothes.

"I'm not sneaking. I didn't think anybody was home. Your car wasn't outside," Essence commented, continuing to throw items in her suitcase.

"My car's getting serviced," Bailey said, sitting down on the bed. "So what's going on with you? You haven't been here for the last couple days, now you look like you're packing for a long extended trip."

"Shiffon didn't tell you what happened?" Essence questioned.

"No. Honestly she's been MIA her damn self. By the time she gets home, I'm usually sleep. This new job she's working seems to be taking up a lot of her time. Does this trip you're packing for have anything to do with Shiffon's new gig?"

"Nope. I'm done with Bad Bitches Only. I'm moving back to North Carolina. Maybe be like you and go back to school," Essence stated.

"Back to school...to study what? I haven't been to a class in weeks." Bailey admitted.

"I knew you took some time off after getting out the hospital but I thought you had been back attending classes?" Essence was surprised by Bailey's disclosure.

"Yeah, I guess you can say I've been faking the funk. I never wanted to attend law school in the first place. It was all Dino's doing. But after what he put me through," Bailey twirled her hair around her finger nervously, looking off in deep thought. "That man beat me within an inch of my life. I just want to feel empowered again and attending law school just ain't doing that," she sighed.

"I feel you. The wrong nigga can have yo' head all

fucked up. Having you question yourself...your sanity. No doubt Dino did a number on you. But you survived. You can't say the same thing about him, he's dead. So you won."

"I ain't won shit. I'm alive physically, but mentally I feel dead."

"Baily, don't talk like that!" Essence shouted becoming concerned.

"I'm not suicidal or anything," Bailey wanted to reassure her, seeing how worried Essence appeared.

"If you haven't been in school, where have you been disappearing to during the day?"

"Going for long walks, sightseeing. Atlanta has so many beautiful tourist spots I've never taken advantage of. I've also been seeing a therapist." Bailey seemed reluctant to divulge.

"Ain't nothing wrong wit' that. You made the right move, especially if it's helping."

"Thanks for saying that, Essence. Initially, seeing a therapist had me thinking I was losing my mind but honestly I was. I kept having these visions of Dino hovering over me with this evil grimace on his face, punching me over and over again. I was waking up in the middle of the night, drenched in sweat."

"Bailey, I'm so, so sorry. I feel like shit for not realizing what you were going through. Does Shiffon know?"

"No. I've been good at keeping things to myself. But seeing the therapist has helped some. It's difficult because of course I don't wanna tell her the part I played in Dino's murder."

"Or that you hired your cousin to do it." Essence cracked.

"That part too," Bailey nodded. "I don't know, I'm just struggling to find my way right now. Enough about that, I need you to tell me why you're bailing on Bad Bitches Only and moving back to North Carolina. I know Shiffon must be devastated."

"Oh please!" Essence scoffed. "Trust me, Shiffon could care less about me moving out or that I'm done with Bad Bitches Only."

"That's not true."

Bailey and Essence both turned towards the doorway entrance and saw Shiffon standing there. There was a long awkward silence as Essence went back to filling her suitcase with clothes and ignoring what Shiffon said.

"Is anybody gonna tell me what the hell is going on?" Bailey stood up and questioned, killing the silence. "What is up between the two of you? Essence moving out and..."

"Essence you leaving?!" Shiffon interrupted Bailey before she could finish her sentence.

"Yep. Maybe now you can let Leila move in." Essence replied with sarcasm.

"Now I'm totally confused...who is Leila?" Bailey wanted to know. "And why is you talking about her moving in?" she questioned, glancing over at Essence.

"Why don't you ask your cousin, since she's her new partner in crime," Essence popped.

"I apologize for keeping you out the loop with what we had planned at the party. I also shouldn't have been so quick to..."

"To what...kick me outta the crew I was the very first member of," Essence popped, tossing down the jeans she was about to put in her suitcase. "We're supposed to be friends and you had no problem dismissing me like I'ma nobody!" She fumed.

"I didn't think of it like that but I'm sorry for not being more considerate of your feelings." Shiffon wanted Essence to know. "I don't want you moving out and I still want you to be a part of Bad Bitches Only. But I also want Leila to be a part of it too. There's room for both of you. That is, if you're willing to be a team player."

"I'm sorry too. I did overreact about the Leila situation. And you're right, I was a little jealous," Essence conceded. Slumping down on the bed.

"You don't have any reason to be jealous. The only reason I chose Leila was because she already had a relationship with Enzo," Shiffon explained again.

"I know and it makes total sense. Honestly, this isn't even about Leila," Essence sighed. "For so long my identity came from being Bezo's girl. Then when he got locked up, I ain't have shit. I ain't feel good about myself. Then we came into some money, you thought of this new assassin gig for us and I started feeling cute again. But seeing Leila with Enzo was a reminder of how much I missed having a man by my side. I know I sound weak as fuck, but everybody ain't strong like you, Shiffon."

"You don't think I was depressed as fuck after Clay got locked up! But I only had two options, either cry myself to sleep every night or figure out how to fuckin' survive. I chose to survive. Latching on to another nigga is the last thing I want. I wanna make my own money and Bad Bitches Only is how I'ma get it. I want you to be on the squad, part of the team but I need yo' mind to be right and not on no bullshit. What do you say?" Shiffon wasn't sure how Essence would respond.

"Let's make this shit happen!" Essence smiled.

"And what about Leila?" Shiffon had to make sure Essence was willing to welcome the new chick too.

"I'm good on Leila too," she nodded.

"And what about me?" Bailey questioned after remaining quiet for the duration of their conversation.

"What about you?" Shiffon and Essence both asked simultaneously.

"What about me joining the squad...where my invite?"

They couldn't tell if Bailey was joking or serious. And Shiffon didn't want to know.

"Anywho, Essence while you're unpacking, I can fill you in on all the latest details regarding Martina and her crew." Shiffon sat down on the chair in the corner.

"So cousin, you just gon' ignore me. I was dead ass serious. I wanna be down too. I think I would make a pretty good assassin. I'm also very creative when it comes to changing up my look," Bailey added.

"There's a lot more to being an assassin then playing dress up, Bailey. For one you can't be afraid to pull the trigger. Even Essence is scared to bust off."

"I ain't scared! I just don't really know how," Essence shrugged. "Everybody's man wasn't teaching them how to handle a weapon."

"I guess Clay deserves the credit for making sure I could shoot my target without hesitation. The point is, I don't think you're up to this, Bailey. This shit can get real ugly," Shiffon emphasized.

"No uglier than what I've been through with Dino." Bailey glanced over at Essence, before putting her head down.

"Shiffon, maybe we should give her a chance," Essence said, thinking about the conversation her and Bailey had a little while ago. "I mean, at least we know we can trust her."

"I can't believe you're cosigning on this." Shiffon started shaking her head in disbelief. "I thought you would be the main one against it. You're always saying what a princess Bailey is. Now you want her to join a group of assassins?!?"

"You call me a princess?" Bailey smacked.

"I say it with love and you do have princess tendencies. I mean where's the lie." Essence was doing her best to downplay it.

"Maybe I did but that was before I danced with the devil. The princess in me died with Dino."

Shiffon felt a chill go down her spine after hearing her cousin speak those words. *Damn, I've been so focused on this new gig. Making sure I deliver everything Alex wants because I don't want to piss him off and he bad mouth me, that I haven't noticed Bailey needs my help,* Shiffon thought to herself.

"Why not," Shiffon finally said to her cousin. "I mean if it wasn't for you, I would've never even came up with the idea. So if anyone deserves an opportunity, it's you, Bailey."

"Shiffon, thank you so much!!" Bailey ran over to her cousin and gave her a hug. "You have no idea how much I need this."

Actually I do. And if this can help you get through whatever demons you're battling, then so be it, Shiffon said to herself. "I do have one mandatory requirement of you and Essence."

"Oh gosh! I shoulda kept my mouth shut." Essence rolled her eyes.

"Well, it's too late now. Plus, the requirement is for the betterment of the organization," Shiffon made clear. "You an Bailey both need to learn how to shoot a gun. It's important you understand at least the basic skills on how to handle a weapon. Like the difference between a revolver and a semi-automatic pistol. Are ya' tryna be real assassins or what?"

"I am!" Bailey quickly said.

"Me too," Essence spoke up.

"Then it's settled." Shiffon clapped her hands together. "Three times a week the two of you will be attending target practice. I know the exact spot. It's very lowkey and the dude who runs it, will teach you everything you need to know."

"Man, I can't believe this is really happening. I'm so excited!" Bailey hugged her cousin again.

Whatever disinclination Shiffon had about welcoming Bailey into the fold disappeared, after seeing that twinkle in her eyes for the first time in months. She believed that sparkle had vanished for good, until now. If giving her cousin a purpose would put a smile back on her face, then Shiffon was game.

Chapter Seven

DEALS AND DILEMMAS

Taz Boy was in the booth dropping bars. The niggas tongue was scorching. Each lyric delivered more fire, as if trying to kill the competition with his coveted gift for wordplay. With all his critical and commercial success, Taz Boy had something to prove and his energy in the studio made that clear.

"You got here right on time. That nigga goin' the fuck off in there," hip hop producer Prize, belted when Alex entered the room.

Alex stayed on mute, not so much as nodding his head to the bangin' beat blaring through each speaker. No one was surprised, that's how he moved... in silence. His tight inner circle gave up a long time ago on trying to figure out what their boss was thinking because people rarely got it right. He had the poker face game on lock. Alex's knack for maintaining a neutral expression, always kept one guessing.

"Let me cut that shit again," Taz Boy said over his mic, feeling himself. Prize was about to start the track again but Alex motioned his hand to end it.

"Come on out. I need to speak with you." Alex directed Taz Boy. He took of his headphones and stepped out the booth.

"What's good, boss." Taz Boy greeted Alex, locking arms with him for a moment.

"You sounding like a champ in there. Very impressive." Alex told his artist, who appreciated the positive feedback. Like most, Taz Boy always valued his input. Follow me into the lounge area, so we can have some privacy," Alex insisted.

I'm right behind you," Taz Boy grinned, feeling optimistic shit was turning in his favor. "So you really feelin' my new music," he stated proudly, sitting down across from Alex in the private lounge area.

"You know I don't hold back. That shit was straight," Alex nodded.

"I put my heart and soul into that shit."

"You always do. It's the reason people fuck wit' you so hard."

"Yeah, but it's different this time. I want this album to really reflect the bullshit I been hit wit' these last few months. After my arrest, muthafuckas really tryna count me out the game. Sayin' I ain't gon' beat the charges and have to do real time. One minute they was singing my praises, next they burying me and my career." Taz Boy was shaking his head in frustration.

"You know this industry is flooded wit' vampires and blood suckers. They fake fucks with no fangs. You can't take that shit personally. It's one of the prices of fame. But you'll bounce back. Just give it a little time." Alex reassured him.

"I feel you but this generation right here gotta short attention span. You have to keep feeding them the goods or they on to the next. But I only got a couple of songs left to record and this new album will be ready for release."

"About that. I think we need to be real strategic with your next release. We need a real strong club banger." Alex stated.

"I feel you. I think I got one of those."

"I was thinking your lead single should feature Enzo. He on top of the charts right now. Radio loving him. The two of you on a joint together is guaranteed to shoot straight to number one."

"I don't need no R&B nigga to go number one!" Taz Boy scoffed. "I get we labelmates but when you release my album, I'm snatching up that number one spot."

"The thing is, we not releasing your album anytime soon."

"Why the fuck not?!" Taz Boy jumped out of his chair.

"Because these federal charges is bleeding your budget dry. None of the sponsors is fuckin' wit you right now. At your bail hearing, per the conditions of your release, you have a lot of travel restrictions, which means you can't tour."

"When I got out, all you kept stressin' was for me to get back in the studio and create new music. That would fix all this shit! Well I did it and now you tellin' me you puttin' my shit on the shelf and gon' let it sit," Taz Boy roared.

"I didn't think the charges was gonna stick. I figured your lawyer would find a way to get them dismissed. Unfortunately, that hasn't happened."

"But I didn't do that shit! Them drugs, those guns wasn't mine. I swear, Alex!" Taz Boy damn near looked like he was about to cry.

"I know and I believe you." Alex placed his hand on Taz Boy's shoulder. "You have to trust me. I'ma fix it but it's gonna take a lot more time. I've always looked out for you. Have I ever advised you wrong?"

"Nah." Taz Boy put his head down.

"I know this ain't what you wanted to hear and you're disappointed. I get it but like I said, you have to trust me," Alex asserted.

"I do. I trust you more than probably anybody I know."

"Good. Then you'll do the song with Enzo?"

"Yeah, If you think it'll help, I'll do it," Taz Boy agreed.

"It will help. Listen, at Fortune Five Records we're a family. When one of us is down, we do whatever's necessary to help you rise again. Right now, Enzo is on top. He's your brother, so it's his obligation to lift you up. Just like you would do the same for him, if he ever had a setback." Alex felt it was imperative he made Taz Boy understand they were a family, and family stick together.

"You right, I would. I guess I always saw myself as the big brother...the superstar. Now here come the new kid taking my place. It's like overnight, Enzo just blew up. Fucked wit' my ego a bit."

"Can't nobody take yo' place.. You earned your position as the biggest rapper in the game right now. You'll do the single with Enzo and then some features with other artist to keep yo' name hot in the streets and on radio. Once you beat those fed charges and all that shit die down, we'll release your new album. You'll be back on top," Alex promised.

Everybody wanna be lit, everybody wanna be rich
Everybody wanna be this, if I was you, I'd hate me bitch
Read my rhymes, nigga, suck my dick
All of that talk and I'm calling it out
Public opinions from private accounts
You not a check, then you gotta bounce
I got the drip, come get an ounce
They do anything for clout (Clout)
They do anything for clout (Whoo)
Bitches is mad, bitches is trash (Errr)
Oscar the Grouch (Grouch)
Seeing me win, they gotta hurt
Ooh, ooh, ouch
Said when they see me, what they gon' do?
Bitch, not from the couch, bah

Martina was spitting Cardi's verse word for word like she wrote the shit, as Offset's song Clout blasted from her new Benz. She was in love with herself, even more than usual while speeding down I-95 in New Jersey, headed towards the George Washington Bridge.

"Man, Cardi rips that verse." Martina bounced in her seat, switching lanes. "She sums up just how I feel about them trolls who be leaving fucked up comments on my Instagram page."

"Okurrr!" Harmony and Martina both burst out laughing. "I saw all those comments them hatin' ass trolls left when you posted the pics of you standing next to yo' new Benz. They was big mad."

"Wasn't they! Swearing down this wasn't my shit," Martina cracked. "I was tempted to tell them ninjas, this whip was courtesy of Enzo, or better yet, Fortune Five Records. I'm on the muthafuckin' payroll now," she bragged.

"I still can't believe you pulled that shit off," Harmony said, applying some more lip gloss.

"I really can't take credit. I mean it was my brilliant idea to go live on Instagram airing Enzo ass out but never did I think doing so would put some real loot in my pocket. I have to give Desi the credit for that," Martina told her friend.

"You might've finally encountered a bitch who slicker than you," Harmony winked. "I wish I would've went to Atlanta wit' ya'll, so I could've met her."

"She'll be in town tomorrow for my birthday celebration, so you can meet her then," Martina beamed.

"The two of you seem to be getting mad close."

"We have a lot in common. Plus she not jealous of me like most females. I guess cause she got her own nigga trickin' on her. She not competing for mine, so the rest of ya better step it up, or Desi will be the only friend I keep in my inner circle," Martina joked but was dead ass serious and Harmony knew it.

Chapter Eight

WELCOME TO BAD BITCHES ONLY

"A'ight ladies, tonight is it," Shiffon said to Bailey and Essence, while double checking her gun was in the purse she was carrying. "Martina's entire little clique should be in attendance at this birthday celebration she's having at her hotel suite. One of them is the informant and our job tonight is to figure out who it is."

"Besides one, I can't imagine any of them gaggling chicks I met at Enzo's party that night, being an FBI informant," Essence shrugged, slipping on her shoes. "My money still on Martina. That heffa would snitch on her own mama, if it got her what she wanted."

"True but all Martina craves is attention and she wants credit for that attention...good or bad. Being an informant would require her to keep her shenanigans a secret. I just don't see her trifling ass agreeing to that," Shiffon rationalized.

"You have a point. Look at the retraction video she posted about Enzo. She had no problem admitting to the fuckin' world she lied on that man, all because she felt like he played her," Bailey pointed out. "Then she tried to flip it like she was still the victim. That hoe is batshit crazy."

"No she's a narcissist," Shiffon countered. "But the real crazy part, is a lot of the comments under the video was people sympathizing with her. I will say this, she didn't delete not one comment where people were trashing her for the filth she is. Martina truly don't give a fuck if you talkin' shit about her, as long as you talking."

"That's because she keeps being rewarded for her stunts. She tried to ruin Enzo's career and then gets a brand new Benz out the deal." Essence rolled her eyes. "I don't know how you got Alex to cut that check for her. Shiiiit, that nigga could've gave me the money to cut her throat instead."

"It was worth it to him. Alex has major plans for Enzo's career. He can't afford to have his name attached to some bullshit. He wasn't happy to write the check but he def didn't have a problem wit' cuttin' it. But I'm sure he would be thrilled if we find out Martina is the informant, so he's justified with having her killed," Shiffon added.

"I bet he will," Essence cracked, checking her appearance in the hallway mirror in their hotel room.

"Is everybody ready to go? I wanna make sure we have ample time to observe these chicks. Alex is getting anxious. He wants results."

"I'm ready." Essence stated.

"Almost," Bailey said, struggling to apply her Luxe Cashmere No. 9 lash to the right eye. "What about Leila? I know she isn't coming to the party with us but are we meeting up with her at some point during the duration of the trip?" she inquired.

"Leila is actually already in New York with Enzo. He's gonna be here for a few days, recording some music and working on an upcoming music video. He wanted to fly her out here and I told her to come," Shiffon explained.

"So Leila is still seeing Enzo...I thought her being his date for the party was for work purposes?" Essence's voice was dripping with sarcasm.

"It was but like I told you, Leila had been dating Enzo for a minute before she joined Bad Bitches Only. Their relationship was an added bonus."

"It seems like the only bonus is for Leila. Instead of working like we are tonight, she jet setting wit' Enzo. How is that benefitting our team?" Essence wanted to know.

"Leila is working. There's no telling what she might come across or find out during some pillow talk with Enzo," Shiffon clarified.

"I doubt much talkin' is going on between the two of them," Essence countered. "Hell, did you ever consider Leila might be the informant?"

Shiffon and Bailey both stopped what they were doing and stared at each other before setting their glare on Essence.

"You did say Alex told you, a bunch of people was at Taz Boy's mansion before the feds raided his crib. Since Leila isn't part of Martina's crew, maybe she wasn't on Alex's radar. But according to you, she's been fuckin' Enzo for a minute, which means she's been in the mix. That gives her opportunity to be a snitch like the rest of them broads." Essence had her hand placed on her hip, like bitches I'll wait for you to point out the lie but there isn't one.

"Essence does have a point." Bailey was the first to acknowledge.

Shiffon was a little more hesitant to add Leila to

the suspect list but she couldn't rule her out either. She also couldn't dispute what Essence said. "You have a valid argument. Alex has always maintained the informant is a chick posing as a clout chaser. Someone who can easily blend in with the bevy of groupies his artists keep around, making it almost impossible to figure out who she is."

"Sounds like Leila to me," Essence said. "I was riding wit' Martina because she was the lowest hanging fruit. Plus, although she doesn't come across as a master manipulator, she's the only one out of the bunch of her not so bright friends, who would have the balls to try and pull it off. Not only that, believes she could get away with it."

"Leila on the other hand is more sneaky with how she moves. People would tend to underestimate her... never see her coming. That quality was the main reason I believed she would be perfect to get at Martina at the party and be an asset to Bad Bitches Only," Shiffon said, sharing her thoughts out loud to Bailey and Essence.

Fuck! Has Leila been playing me this entire time. Have I been wasting all my energy kissing up to Martina, when the real snake has been breaking bread with me at the table. If Essence is right, then I'm screwed. Those thoughts, Shiffon kept to herself. She wasn't ready to share just how bad this would be if it turned out Leila was the one who set Taz Boy up.

"Bitch, you lookin' like a snack!" Harmony complimented Martina on the sultry, satin fuchsia dress she was wearing. The chiffon contrast side with crochet lace detail, invisible back zipper and just enough stretch in the fabric to highlight her best assets and conceal the not so flattering ones, would make this dress any girl's favorite.

"Thanks babe!" Martina beamed, blowing Harmony a kiss. "As soon as I slipped it on, I knew I'd be wearing it for my birthday. It does look amazing on me!" She boasted, taking a sip of champagne straight from the bottle. Martina planned on carrying a bottle of bubbly around all night. Determined to get drunk and stay drunk.

"Martina is on ten tonight and the party just got started," Flora commented to Kayla, while fixing herself a small plate from the food Martina had catered.

"Fuck ten, more like one hundred," Tish said, overhearing Flora's comment.

"It is her birthday you all. She deserves to have some fun," Kayla remarked, remaining team Martina. Kayla didn't agree with a lot of choices Martina made but she was quick to make excuses for her behavior, due to her admiration for the unapologetic fame chaser.

"Please, it being her birthday has nothing to do with it. She loves showing out," Flora shot back.

"Don't you mean showing off," Tish giggled.

"Yeah, that too," Flora agreed.

"Are you bitches over here talking shit about me!" Martina walked up on them out the blue. The ladies thought they had been caught until Martina began laughing hysterically. "I'm only kidding you morons!" She continued to laugh. "I know ya'll ain't dumb enough to talk shit about me, especially at my own fuckin' party," she said, shoving each of them on the shoulder.

"Of course we knew you were joking, Martina!" Kayla smiled. "You know how much we all love you. You our Queen B!" She gushed.

Heffa, speak for yourself. Martina's self absorbed ass ain't my Queen B, Flora thought to herself, biting down on her shrimp cocktail.

If Kayla believed her fawning would inspire Martina to give her some attention, she would be waiting by the buffet table all night. Because the moment Shiffon walked through the door, she forgot about everyone else in the room.

"Desi! You made it My Love!" Martina gave Shiffon a huge embrace and then started placing sloppy wet kisses all over her face. The liquor was now floating in her system strong, so Martina was oblivious to how annoying she was being but it wasn't like she would care anyway.

"Happy Birthday gorgeous!" Shiffon beamed, handing Martina a beautifully wrapped present.

"Omifuckingoodness! You got me a present! None of these other bitches did." Martina slurred her words while opening the small jewelry box in the middle of the hotel suite. "These are stunning." Her eyes expanded with excitement, staring at the earrings. "They real diamonds too not them bullshit diamond chips," she continued, pulling them close to her eyes to analyze. "There ain't no visible yellowish color either," she said noticing how the diamonds were refracting and dispersing lots of light. "Thank you so, so much!" She held Shiffon tightly.

"You welcome. I'm glad you like them."

"I don't fuckin' like them...I love them! I'll be right back. I'ma go to the bathroom and take these hoops off and put these on," she smiled.

"That went well," Bailey giggled.

"Yeah, I thought her ass what 'bout to give you some pussy right here," Essence cracked.

"You crazy," Shiffon laughed. "But enough wit' the jokes. Let's grab some drinks, go sit down and start sizing up these clout chasers."

Shiffon, Essence and Bailey spent the next couple hours scrutinizing every chick they laid eyes on. It got to a point the lace frontals, cut crease eye shadow makeup and Instagram boutique outfits all started looking identical. It was like every woman in the room was following the same blueprint. So instead of discovering clues to help them zero in on the imposter, they were left even more dumbstruck.

"I hate to admit this but maybe Essence is right. Leila is who we should be targeting." Shiffon mumbled in a low tone to Bailey.

"I heard that." Essence reached her arm across Bailey's lap and lightly hit Shiffon's leg.

"Listen, I have no problem admitting when I'm wrong," Shiffon stated. "This is the first time I've been around Martina and her entire crew, together in a small setting. All I'm seeing is dumb, dumber and the dumbest. I can't imagine any of these vain broads giving up one second of their day, let alone hours to sit down with a federal agent. They're taking selfies every five minutes and between selfies, they're retouching their makeup. The only person they're obsessed with is themselves. What carat could the feds possibly be dangling, to pull one of them away from a camera phone and great filter? Serious question?"

"You gets no argument from me," Essence popped.

"Well, coming from the prospective of someone who loves taking selfies and watching a great cut crease tutorial, I probably can relate to these ladies more than the two of you," Bailey confirmed. "I'm guessing the only thing that could motivate one of them to step out their comfort zone, would be for a nigga wit' a lot of paper or some fame. So, I have to agree with Essence. My money's on Leila too."

Before Shiffon could give her final thoughts on

the Leila situation, the birthday girl made an announcement. The celebration was now moving from her hotel suite to 10ak, a club in Chelsea near the Meatpacking District.

"Now that sounds like fun!" Baily said with enthusiasm. "I've heard of that club. It's supposed to be one of the trendiest and most exclusive clubs in New York City. It's known for its famous guests and afterparties following big events like Fashion Week and music award shows. At least that's what they say in the blog world."

"Thanks for the insight," Shiffon nodded. "But remember we're still on the clock."

"Oh goodness, here we go again." Essence frowned up her face. "The long ass sermon about we here to work and not have fun."

"Our work is done." Bailey raised an eyebrow. "I thought we were all in agreement that Leila is now our target. We've already wasted half our night on watch patrol, now it's time to have some fun."

"Listen ladies. I'm not completely convinced Leila is the one and until I am, we have a job to do. This isn't the time to put your guard down. Every chick in this room is still on our radar. Now let's go," Shiffon ordered, snatching her purse from the chair.

"Is she always this uptight?" Bailey whispered to Essence as they followed behind Shiffon.

"When she's working...always. Welcome to Bad Bitches Only!"

Chapter Nine

AT THE CLUB

When the ladies arrived at 453 W 17th Street, there would be no waiting for the birthday girl and her gaggle of groupie friends. Martina's friend Stacey was fucking one of the front door bouncers, so there was no line, no wait, just immediate entrance into the club. The stylish and chic interior was exactly what one might envision a celebrity hotspot would resemble.

The women were led to two large booths that could accommodate them.

Although money didn't seem to be an issue tonight, Shiffon did her part in keeping Martina as her biggest cheerleader. She quickly purchased a few bottles of overpriced champagne. A couple for each table. With the bubbly popping and the music blasting, the ladies were all lit. It was about to be the ultimate girls night out until Enzo and his posse showed up. To make matters worse, Leila was draped on his arm like a fine piece of jewelry. The mocha snake print jumpsuit with spaghetti straps, skinny leg and padded bra, with a long fishtail braid decorated with a trail of hair rings for extra dimension, had Leila looking like a Glamazon. Shiffon was hoping Martina's buzz was still going strong and she didn't notice the couple walk in.

"Oh shit! Isn't that Leila," Bailey said, smacking her cousin's hand.

"Yeah, but don't look in their direction," Shiffon stated. "I'm hoping Martina didn't see them." She glanced over at the other booth where Martina was seated to see if her mood changed. She appeared to be upbeat and in a zone. "I think we might be good."

"Are you gonna go say anything to Leila?" Bailey asked.

"Hell nah! She's supposed to be the enemy...remember. Martina would have a fit if she saw me over there talking to the chick that was about to drag her across the floor," Shiffon said, glancing down at her phone. “Oh, I’ll be right back! This is Binky calling. It might be about a potential new client.”

The music was blasting so loud, Shiffon was almost halfway out the door before she could hear anything. “Binky, can you hear me now?”

“Yeah. I can hear you. You in town?”

“Nope, I’ll be back in a couple days.”

“Work or business?”

“Business nigga, why?”

“Somebody wants to meet with you and the pay is real good,” Binky stressed.

“Excellent but I’m not finish working this one assignment.”

“Word...you still on that same job! It’s lasting a mighty long time.” Binky stated in his deep southern drawl.

“It’s taking a little longer than I anticipated but I’m ‘bout to wrap it up.”

“Good. Cause you don’t wanna leave no money on the table. Muthafuckas quick to say adios, when you take too long. Niggas don’t like being placed on hold. They ain’t tryna wait. Fuck around and they do that shit themselves.”

“I hear you, Binky.” Shiffon wasn’t in the mood for the don’t leave no money on the table lecture from Binky. She knew he was right but his concern was about him getting his finder fee percentage, not niggas level of patience.

“Is that music playin’? You out partying? Ain’t you

supposed to be workin'. How you in the club shakin' yo' ass, when you on an assignment?"

"If you must know, my assignment has me at the club right now, so I am working!" Shiffon shot back.

"A'ight then. Carry on. But hit me as soon as you touch back down in the A."

"Will do. Bye."

I guess this nigga be thinking he Charlie and we Charlie's Angels. Like nah nigga, we don't work for you. This my shit. You just gettin' a cut, Shiffon said, to herself as she walked back to their table. "Girl, pour me a drink," she said to Bailey, sitting back down. "Binky tryna add to this headache I already have."

"Hopefully this glass of champagne will do the trick and take away that stress," Bailey smiled, handing her cousin the glass she filled up to the rim.

"Thanks." Shiffon let out a long deep sigh. Leaning back on the leather cushion, enjoying the sweet taste of alcohol. "Wait." Shiffon sat up straight in her seat and focused. "Where did Martina and the rest of the girls sitting at her table go?"

"I'm not sure. I was dancing and drinking. I wasn't paying them no mind." Bailey turned and nudged Essence on the shoulder. She too was caught up in the music and drinks. "Do you know where Martina and them went?" she asked.

"Nope!"

Shiffon then glanced over at the table where Enzo and his crew was seated. Although Leila was the only female with them, at first it was difficult for Shiffon to see because there were so many people in his group. Once she got a better look, Shiffon realized Leila was nowhere to be found.

"Oh fuck! I'll be right back!" Shiffon said, rushing off.

"Where you going?!" Bailey called out but her cousin was ghost.

"Can you tell me where the bathroom is?" Shiffon asked some random woman she walked past. The lady pointed her in the right direction and she made a beeline to the restroom. Shiffon took a deep breath and her gut instinct was right. When she opened the door, Martina and four of her friends were trying to beat Leila down. They jumped her but even with the mob of women, Leila was holding her own. She had taken off her shoes, and was swinging on them bitches barefoot.

Shiffon's initial reaction was to run in there and just start whopping ass. But she had to think strategically. If she made that move, her cover would instantly be blown. Shiffon knew she had to do something though and fast. Leila could fight but nobody would be able to withstand five angry birds trying to stomp you out at the same damn time.

Think Shiffon...think! You can't stand by and let them chicks beat the shit out of Leila but you can't go in there and jump on them either. Shiffon argued with herself unable to decide what her next move should be until she came up with an idea. Under the circumstances, she felt it was the best alternative. Shiffon found a crowd of people who were obviously drunk and dancing wildly. She joined them and started dancing too. Everyone was so lit, that no one noticed when she pulled out her gun and shot up in the air three times. Making sure everyone heard it.

The crowd went crazy. Panic consumed the dancefloor. While everyone was screaming and running for cover, Shiffon ran back to the bathroom. "Martina come on! Somebody's shooting in the club. We have to get outta here!" She screamed at the top of her lungs."

"I told you I heard gunfire!" Tish shouted to no one in particular.

"Come on! Come on! Let's go!" Shiffon grabbed Martina's arm because she knew once the ringleader started leaving, the rest would follow. Shiffon locked eyes with Leila for a brief moment and gave her an intense stare, making sure she was alright. Leila nodded her head to acknowledge she was hurt but straight and it was okay for her to go.

Man, if I don't figure this shit out soon, I'ma gather these hoes up and just put each of them out they misery. At this point, I'd rather they all be dead than deal with these theatrics again, Shiffon fussed to herself as they made their way out the club.

Chapter Ten

TIC TOC...YOUR TIME IS UP

Leila woke up in pain but it wasn't from getting dick downed by Enzo, it was from brawling in the bathroom at the club. She rolled over and saw him sitting up on the edge of the bed.

"You finally woke up," Enzo said with a half smirk

on his face. "Even wit' that cut under yo' eye, you still look cute." He then placed a kiss on Leila's forehead. "You sure you don't want me to have somebody take you to the hospital. Or I can have a doctor come to the room," he offered.

"Damn, I look that fucked up?" Leila questioned, scared to see her reflection in the mirror.

"Nah, I told you, you still look cute but gettin' jumped ain't no fun. A muthafucka could've bruised yo' rib or some shit."

"Yeah, but I don't think it's nothing some aspirin can't fix."

"You lucky somebody started shooting in the club because them crazy broads was probably tryna kill you in there," Enzo shook his head.

"You ain't telling no lies. Martina must miss the dick a lot more than she's willing to admit," Leila laughed.

"Yo, she's ridiculous wit' it. Let me go take this shower. You wanna join me?" Enzo questioned, looking down at his phone.

"Nah, I think I'ma rest a little longer but I'll be ready for you later on."

"I'm countin' on it," he said while replying to a text. "Maybe you can give me some head before I step out to this meeting."

"Then you better hurry up and go take that shower then," Leila teased, licking her lips before biting down on it seductively.

Enzo put down his phone and headed to the bathroom, not giving a second thought that Leila might decide to be nosey. Because she always played it cool, calm and collective, never harassing him or asking a million questions like most of the chicks he fucked with, Enzo had become very comfortable with her...too comfortable.

Leila hurried and grabbed Enzo's phone before it locked because she hadn't figured out his passcode yet. Something about the expression on his face, made her curious as to who he was texting. "This explains it all," she mumbled looking at the naked picture some chick had just sent him.

Daddy I need the dick was the message the woman sent under her image. Leila was tempted to text the chick back and say go suck a dick because Enzo's dick is mine for at least the next couple days but luckily she didn't give into her emotions. She knew they were far from exclusive and he had a gang of broads he was dealing with. But that didn't stop her from catching feelings.

Why does this chick look so familiar to me? Leila wondered dissecting every inch of the woman's face and body. *Maybe she one of those Instagram models and I've seen her on somebody's page,* she thought to herself, staring at a distinctive tattoo on her shoulder. It was a cat eye.

Enzo's slick ass don't even put names to the phone numbers, only emojis, Leila laughed to herself.

"Let me put this man's phone down before I drive myself crazy. I ain't 'bout to become Martina 2.0 over some good dick," she promised herself, laying down and falling back to sleep.

"I'm so ready to pack my shit and go the fuck home!" Shiffon had been ranting and raving these sentiments since she woke up this morning. It was now the middle of the afternoon and nothing had changed. She was furious with how everything went down last night and the only person she blamed was herself.

"I get you mad but we can't go home until the job is done. I mean isn't that what you always say," Essence mocked.

"Cute...real cute, Essence. Maybe if you and Bailey had been on your job, paying attention to Martina and her friends, I wouldn't have had to bust shots in the club!" She seethed.

"Oh, so that's what you really mad about? It ain't my fault we dealing wit' a bunch of savages. How was I supposed to know, them broads would go all guerilla warfare," Essence scoffed

"She's right, Shiffon. None of us was expecting a surprise attack," Bailey said, trying to defend herself.

"The thing is, I was. I specifically said, I wanted to make sure Martina didn't see Enzo come in with Leila.

If it wasn't for that fuckin' Binky calling me, I would've never left the booth and could've prevented all the bullshit from going down," Shiffon fussed.

"Would've...could've...should've," Essence spat, rolling her eyes. "Girl, give it up. You can't make stupid, make sense. Martina and her friends are some loose cannons. It's not yo' job to babysit a bunch of grown heathens."

"But it is! That's what Alex is paying us for!" Shiffon retorted.

"No! Alex is paying us to find the informant and I'm convinced we have. Shiiiit, maybe you shoulda let Martina and her gang of vultures finish Leila off. Then our job would be complete and we could go the fuck home," Essence shrugged, as she continued filing her nails.

"I'm not completely sold Leila is guilty," Shiffon admitted.

"What's changed? I thought that was a done deal?" Bailey questioned.

"Nothing has changed, it's a feeling in my gut. I'm meeting up with Leila in a couple hours while Enzo is laying some tracks at the studio. Before I meet with her, I'm going to see Alex. I just found out he's in town too," Shiffon sighed.

"Now we get why you over there hyperventilating. You gotta check in with the client." Essence stated.

"Yeah, a very unhappy client. He's spent a ton of money and I have nothing to give him. And don't even think about suggesting I mention Leila. Until I know for sure, I'm not going there."

"How do you plan on doing that? It's not like Leila is gonna come out and admit the shit," Bailey said.

"I know. I'ma put somebody on her. Twenty-four hour surveillance. Clock her every move. Of course it can't be one of us because Leila thinks she's a member of the crew. I have somebody in mind but it's gonna be costly. Now all I have to do is convince Alex to open up his wallet one more time." That was one conversation Shiffon wasn't looking forward to having.

"I don't envy your task," Bailey proclaimed. "These type of situations makes me happy I'm just a paid member of Bad Bitches Only and I don't own it."

'Thanks." Shiffon huffed, giving Bailey the sour face. "Essence, at this moment I would give anything for your original guess to be right."

"You mean Martina. Hell, that heffa done did so much dirt, you can easily claim she's the informant and go ahead and kill her. Nobody but maybe her delusional followers would care. To ease your conscious, tell yourself it was done for the greater good," Essence proposed.

"If only it was that easy. Women like Martina are hard to kill. They seem to have more lives than cats," Shiffon cracked.

"My seven day birthday bash just keeps getting better!" Martina boasted, talking to Tish on the phone while getting dressed at the same time. "But so far, nothing has been more fun than watching Enzo's bitch getting stomped on the bathroom floor," she laughed.

"Yo, that shit was crazy. I'm glad Harmony pointed her out and said we should follow her to the bathroom."

"Yep. Best suggestion silly ass Harmony has ever made. What's funny is she thought we were just gonna go in the bathroom and talk shit. Did you see the panic in Harmony's eyes when I took my champagne glass and swung it at Leila."

"Fuck yeah! Harmony weak ass wasn't ready for that. She looked mad scared. You woulda thought you swung the glass at her scary ass," Tish joked.

"Exactly! But that Leila bitch lucky her reflex was fast or that glass woulda fucked her face up."

"Damn straight. I was starting to get some good licks in too but some dumbass had to fuck it up by shooting up the club. Did they ever find out who that was?" Tish asked.

"Nope. I spoke to Stacey about an hour ago and that bouncer she fuck wit' at the club said they have no idea. It was so many people in the area the shots came from, the security cameras didn't get shit," Martina informed her.

"Well did anybody get shot?"

"Nah. Just a bunch of wasted bullets. But boo, I gotta go. I don't wanna be late for my date," Martina said, rushing to get off the phone.

"You still ain't told me who this mystery date is. Do share," Tish pressed.

"All I'll say is it's a juicy one," Martina giggled. "Since you my girl, I'll call you later on tonight and give you all the details but only if I ain't too busy gettin' my back blown out...Bye girl!"

Martina hung up, excited about her dinner date. She would've preferred he pick her up but understood why he wanted the privacy. So she grabbed her purse and left her hotel room, anxious to meet him. Martina wanted to make sure she was on time. She was tempted to tell him they should skip dinner and go back to his place. Getting fucked was her real objective anyway.

Nah, bitch you lookin' too fuckin' cute in this outfit. Titties and ass sittin' right. Let that nigga take you out and show you off, Martina thought to herself as she crossed the street. She was supposed to meet him on the corner but didn't see his car. She kept walking until Martina heard someone blow their horn. She turned to the right, then left and noticed the headlights flashing on a Rolls-Royce Silver Cloud II. "Ahh shit, that nigga pulled out the super expensive shit tonight," Martina beamed walking towards the car. "He definitely want the pussy."

Martina's excitement was about to start making her run towards the vehicle, even though she wearing six-inch heels but she opted against it, not wanting to appear too desperate. Instead she took her time, choosing not to perspire in the hot temperature. She figured she'd wait and sweat her weave out while doing splits on his dick.

"Hey baby! I know you miss this ass," Maritina said knocking on the dark tinted window. "What the fuck?!" she gasped when the driver side window slowly rolled down. It was the last words Martina ever spoke. Unlike last night, not one bullet was wasted, as all four shots laid her to rest. Once the job was done, the Rolls Royce drove off into the night.

Chapter Eleven

LET THE CHIPS FALL

Shiffon's mind was all over the place. She had to push back meeting with Leila because Alex kept changing when he could see her. After multiple time changes, she was keeping her fingers crossed there wouldn't be another. Shiffon pulled up in front of his luxury apartment building and handed the key to her rental car to valet.

Stop being so fuckin' nervous! Shiffon screamed to herself as she rode up the private elevator to Alex's top floor apartment. *My ass need to be nervous. This man has the clout to make or break my business. If word gets out I couldn't deliver the goods, people will be reluctant to hire Bad Bitches Only. Besides my mother and little brother, this company is all I have,* Shiffon thought to herself, watching the elevator door open to another ridiculously opulent crib. *This nigga got all the money...*

"Alex hi," Shiffon smiled warmly.

"Good evening." Alex returned the warm smile, which Shiffon wasn't expecting. She had prepared herself for an heated showdown that included some yelling and even a few thin veiled threats. "I apologize for rescheduling so many times but I couldn't get away from the studio. I had both Taz Boy and Enzo in there recording a new record. Let's just say when you have two superstars competing for the mic, it can get tense," Alex explained.

"I can only imagine but really no apology necessary," Shiffon said, wondering if she should go ahead and request the additional money now, for the surveillance detail on Leila. She figured she should take advantage of Alex's upbeat mood, since it was certain to change once she revealed the case had stalled.

"I guess you're waiting for me to ask before giving me the excellent news," Alex said handing Shiffon a glass of wine.

"Excellent news..." Right after Shiffon said those words a text popped up on her phone.

Martina was murdered. Shot dead less than an hour ago...

The text message from Essence made Shiffon light headed. At least she knew why Alex was in such a good mood. "You must be talking about Martina's death..." She felt a lump in her throat.

"What else would I be talking about. I had a feeling Martina was the snake but now it's been confirmed. I will say, I would've preferred you not leave her bullet ridden dead body in the middle of a New York City street but hey, you got the job done, so I can't really complain," Alex grinned.

Shiffon dreaded what she had to say next. She took a deep breath before she erased that smile off Alex's face. He was actually very pleasant looking and not so intimidating when he was in a cheerful mood. *Stop procrastinating and get it over with already!* Shiffon said to herself before finally speaking.

"Yes, Martina is dead but I had nothing to do with her murder and honestly I don't know who did."

There went the pleasant smile and the familiar grimace stare instantly appeared. "Excuse me?"

"Alex, I'm shocked by Martina's unexpected death. And honestly, I don't think she's the informant. Whoever killed her, it had nothing to do with the job you hired me for," Shiffon conceded.

"What the fuck did I hire you for anyway? So much time and money has been spent, I fuckin' forgot! Remind me again." Alex barked.

"I get your upset but I'm working on a new lead. I just need a little more time."

"I don't have any more time to give you. This should've been handled."

"You're right but it was more complicated than I originally thought. Please Alex. All I'm asking is for a few more days." Shiffon could see his reluctance, so she made the executive decision not to request the additional funds. She would have to find another way to vet Leila.

"Two days. That's all I'm giving you, Shiffon. After that, all bets are off. Now you can show yourself out." Alex turned his back on Shiffon and she knew that meant the conversation was over.

It had been a full twenty-four hours since Martina's murder and Shiffon was still stunned. She felt a gamut of emotions. Martina had a laundry list of despicable qualities but she was so young and there was always a chance she could change her ways, even if it was only a slight one. Now she would never have an opportunity and that saddened Shiffon. But she had too many more important issues to deal with, then to shed one single tear for Martina.

"A'ight ya, now listen," Shiffon said, glancing down at her watch. "Leila should be here any minute. Remember, we're not gonna come at her like we suspect her of anything. We're gonna keep shit real cute. But when I nod at you Essence, that's when you start interrogating her and accusing her of being the informant."

"I still don't understand why I gotta play bad cop," Essence was resistant to the idea.

"Well because Leila already knows you don't like her, so you grilling her will seem believable," Shiffon countered and kept the conversation moving. "Bailey, after Essence grills her for a couple minutes, I'll then nod towards you and you jump in to defend Leila. Then you and Essence start arguing and I'll play peacemaker. Try to be diplomatic. Ask Leila to simply come clean if she's been hiding anything. If she still doesn't break under the pressure, we'll just go with plan B."

"What's plan B?" Bailey seemed confused and so did Essence.

"Simply beat it outta her," Shiffon then turned towards the door when she heard a knock. "Okay, that must be Leila. You guys ready?" she asked. Essence and Bailey both nodded yes and Shiffon went to open the door.

"Hey." Leila said with a slight smile on her face but her energy level was really low.

"Come on in. Is everything okay? You seem a bit down," Shiffon commented.

"Get ready, this is gonna sound crazy but I'm in shock over Martina's death. I couldn't stand that bitch, especially after her and her friends jumped me in the bathroom but it's weird knowing she'll longer be around to drive everyone crazy. Bizarre right," Leila shrugged, putting her purse on the table and sitting down on the sofa near Bailey.

"I think we all feel that way," Bailey agreed. "She was like that annoying nemesis, you figured would always be around causing trouble."

"Well she ain't around!" Essence snapped. "I ain't 'bout to participate in a pity party over trifling ass Martina. Fuck that hexanbeast, moving on."

"I agree. We have bigger problems than Martina," Shiffon said. "I met with Alex last night and he's ready to fire us and I can't blame him. That's why I called this meeting, so we can brainstorm on what we should do to salvage this. Any suggestions?" Shiffon put the question out there and waited for feedback. Her, Bailey and Essence each glanced at each other, hoping Leila would speak up but she was too absorbed in her phone. "Is there something in your phone more important than what I'm talking about right now...if so do share?"

"I'm so sorry, Shiffon. I follow a few people on Instagram who also follow Martina and a lot them are sharing photos that her friends posted," Leila explained.

"Ok! Did we just not say we got more important

things to discuss than Martina's ass!" Essence popped.

"Yeah but a few of the pics are group shots from the night of her birthday party, before they jumped me of course and I know one of these chicks," Leila said, showing the image to Bailey who was sitting right next to her.

"I remember her but I can't think of her name right now," Bailey said, passing Leila's phone to Essence to see if she knew, but she brushed her off.

"Let me see the picture," Shiffon said walking over to them. "That's Harmony. So you know her... from where and why is it important?" she questioned.

"Because Harmony is fuckin' Enzo," Leila told them.

"Are you sure...how do you know?"

"The other day, Enzo reacted a little strange to a text he received. When he went to take a shower, I decided to be nosey. This chick right here sent Enzo a naked picture saying something along the lines that Daddy I need or miss the dick. Something to that affect," Leila revealed.

"And you're positive it was Harmony? I mean I'm sure Enzo has tons of naked women in his phone," Shiffon retorted, unconvinced.

"I'm positive. It was the day after they jumped me in the bathroom. When I saw her pic, I thought she looked familiar but assumed she was just some random Instagram model. But I remember the tattoo on her shoulder, it was a cat eye. The same cat eye, this chick has!" Leila held up her phone again, zooming in on one of the photos where Harmony was turned to the side. She was wearing a strapless dress that easily made her distinctive tattoo visible.

"So wait, Harmony was seeing Enzo. She had to be doing it behind Martina's back. There's no way she would've ever been cool with that. For the brief time I knew here, it was obvious Martina was extremely territorial." Shiffon stated as the wheels began spinning in her head.

"Fine, let's say Harmony was screwing Enzo behind Martina's back. What does sharing dick have to do with us finding the informant?" Essence asked.

"I'm not sure but something is telling me there's some sort of connection. It's just a feeling," Shiffon said.

"Shiffon, you told us, Alex is ready to pull the plug. We're already working on borrowed time. I really don't think we have the luxury of you following a feeling," Essence stressed.

"I have to agree with, Essence." Bailey nodded.

"Tell me something I don't know. When do you not agree with Essence," Shiffon mocked. "Luckily what I think, trumps it all. Everybody get your stuff and lets go," she ordered.

"Where are we going?" Bailey asked, grabbing her purse.

"To go have a conversation with Harmony," Shiffon informed them.

"You know where she lives?" Leila questioned.

"Why do you sound surprised? Of course I know where she lives. One of the first things I did when we got hired for this job, was get an address on Martina and each of her friends. Now let's go because what I do agree with Essence about, is we're working on borrowed time, so we have none to waste." Shiffon put on her sunglasses and the women headed out the door.

Chapter Twelve

HOW DID I GET HERE

When the ladies pulled up to Harmony's townhouse in Hoboken, New Jersey they wasted not a second banging on the door.

"I don't think she's home," Bailey announced.

"Really...how observant of you," Shiffon rolled her

eyes. "It doesn't matter. I'm prepared to stay glued to these stairs until she shows up."

"You don't have to wait much longer. That's her pulling up now." Leila was the first to notice Harmony parking her BMW truck.

Harmony was enthralled in a phone conversation, so it wasn't until she reached the halfway mark did she even see the women waiting for her.

"Let me call you back," Harmony said, ending her call. "Desi, what are you doing here and why are you with her?" she glanced at Leila, feeling salty.

"We needed to speak with you regarding Martina." Shiffion said.

"What about Martina? Of course we're all devastated," Harmony said, brushing past the women, making her way to the front door.

"Why are you in such a rush?" Leila shouted.

"I don't have to tell you anything! Why are you even here...you weren't a friend of Martina!"

"And apparently neither were you," Leila snapped, yanking Harmony's arm. "Did Martina know you were fuckin' Enzo behind her back?!"

All the color drained from Harmony's face and she jerked her arm out of Leila's grasp. Then she did the most unexpected thing. Harmony took off running.

"Yo, these hoes are officially crazy. Did this bitch just take off running." Shiffon stood perplexed. "Man she 'bout to make me run after her silly ass." And that's what Shiffon did. She kicked off her heels and ran down the block flatfoot.

"I've known Shiffon my entire life and never knew my cousin could run that fast. Like she should've ran track in high school," Bailey told Leila and Essence while they watched from the sidelines as Shiffon caught up to Harmony and tackled her like a football player.

"I guess we should go assist her," Essence figured, so the three of them headed up the street.

"Now ya'll decide to show up," Shiffon huffed, sitting on top of Harmony, out of breath. "I swear, the second I get back to Atlanta I'm taking that high intensity circuit Fit9 class I heard muthafuckas swear by," she sighed. "Bailey, pull the car over here." Shiffon reached into her back pocket for the car key and tossed it to her cousin. "Harmony, we're about to take you for a nice, long drive."

The women drove to an empty warehouse Alex had in the outskirts of New York City. By this time it was pitch black with only the headlights from the car and some flashlights they stopped to get before the ride, allowing them to see.

"I think sleeping beauty woke up," Leila said, when they heard pounding coming from the car trunk.

"Good. Right on time." Shiffon was pleased. "I'm gonna get things set up in the warehouse. I'll call you when I'm ready for you all to bring Harmony in."

It took Shiffon less than fifteen minutes to get the chair, ropes and what she described as her bag of goodies out on display. When Essence, Leila and Bailey came in with Harmony, they were taken aback by the torture devices Shiffon had set up.

"Girl, you might be taking this assassin thing way too seriously." Essence was feeling a bit petrified.

And so was Harmony. Her mouth was covered but there was no hiding the fear in her eyes. But Shiffon didn't come to play. She kept thinking about the forty-eight hours Alex gave her and those hours were quickly slipping away.

"Harmony, I'm gonna ask you one time. If you don't start talking and tell me the truth, the torture will begin. And I promise, it won't be pretty. Did you have anything to do with the feds raiding Taz Boy's mansion and did that incident have anything to do with Martina's murder? Leila, remove the tape from her mouth."

"Who are you and why are you doing this to me?!" Harmony sobbed uncontrollably.

"You're stupid and hardheaded. Leila, put the tape back over her mouth."

Shiffon made good on her promise. She had the ladies help her implement what was known as a Palestinian hanging. They hung Harmony with her arms behind her head which caused the arms to dislocate from their sockets. This also would make it difficult for her to breathe.

"Goodness, I feel sorry for her. That looks painful." Bailey shook her head.

"Shiffon, you're a fuckin' genius!" Was Leila's response to the matter.

But Shiffon wasn't done yet. She grabbed one of her goodies off the table. It was a device called a Picana. It's designed to give electric shocks during torture. Shiffon stood on top of a chair in front of Harmony and ripped off the tape. Shiffon could barely see Harmony's eyes because her tears had smeared all her makeup.

"Are you ready to answer my questions, or are you ready to die?"

"I'll talk...I'll talk!" Harmony bawled. "I'll tell you anything you want to know, just please put me down!" She begged.

Shiffon granted her request and allowed Harmony to sit down in a chair. Not wanting to endure anymore torture, she held nothing back. Once Harmony began sharing the diabolical tale, Shiffon felt compelled to pull out her phone and get Harmony's confession on camera. Because you would literally have to see it to believe it.

Chapter Thirteen

ON TOP OF THE WORLD

Early the next afternoon Shiffon headed over to Alex's apartment. By the time they finished up with Harmony and got back to the city, it was two o'clock in the morning. Plus, after the crazy night they had, Shiffon needed a goodnight sleep before having to deliver the devastating news to Alex.

"Shiffon, if you came over to ask for more time, you're not getting it. When I said forty-eight hours that's what I meant."

"And good afternoon to you too, Alex. Is that how you greet all your guests?" Shiffon mimicked.

"I thought we were past formalities," he said closing the door.

"I suppose you're right and no I don't need more time," Shiffon said, cutting to the chase.

Alex stopped mid step and turned towards Shiffon who was still standing in the foyer entrance of his apartment. "What are you saying...did you find out who the informant is?" he seemed almost hesitant to ask the question, not wanting to set himself up for disappointment. Alex had pretty much resigned himself to accepting Shiffon wasn't capable of getting the job done.

"Yes, I can confirm I know who is responsible for setting up Taz Boy but she wasn't an informant for the FBI."

"I'm not following you. What do you mean she wasn't an informant?"

"She did leave the drugs and guns at his house and played a role in setting Taz Boy up but it wasn't because she was working for the FBI."

"Then why?"

"I'm going to let you hear it for yourself."

Shiffon pulled out her phone and had Alex sit down. The video was extra-long, so she fast forwarded to where the most important part started.

"I was in love with Enzo. I would've done anything for him," Harmony confessed through a flood of tears. "He was unhappy with how his music career was going. He had all the talent but felt the bulk of the money was going towards promoting Taz Boy because he was the record label's superstar. He figured if Taz Boy got into some serious legal trouble, it would force the label to put him on the backburner and push Enzo and his upcoming album instead. It worked too," she laughed nervously.

"So how does all that tie into Martina's death?" Shiffon asked her.

"Enzo has this thing of leaving his phone around. After I left the drugs and guns at Taz Boy's house, I sent Enzo a text message letting him know it was done. Martina was with him and saw the text. She didn't know it was from me, because Enzo uses emojis for phone numbers instead of actual names. But once news hit of Taz Boy's arrest, Martina sorta put everything together and knew Enzo played a major role in what happened."

"Did Enzo have any idea Martina knew?"

"Not at first. In typical Martina fashion, she kept the information in her back pocket to use as a weapon to get what she wants and she wanted Enzo. After that incident at his party with her over there," Harmony cut her eyes at Leila. "Martina was furious. It only got worse after she made that video lying on him. She thought all those silly tactics would get Enzo's attention and he would start fuckin' with her again but he didn't."

"So what did Martina do?"

"She finally pushed Enzo too far. After they jumped Leila at the club, the next day Martina called him. She told Enzo she knew it was him that set up Taz Boy and threatened to post a video on her Instagram letting the world know."

"Unless he did what...pay her off?" Shiffon questioned.

"When it came to Enzo, it wasn't about the money for Martina. She wanted him back. He agreed to see her. That night, she got all dressed up thinking Enzo was taking her out to dinner. But it wasn't him waiting in the car, it was me," Harmony confessed.

"You shot and killed Martina?" even through the video you could hear the loud gasps in the warehouse when Harmony divulged that bit of info. She looked like she was afraid to break a nail, let alone pull a trigger. Harmony was a prime example of never judging a book by its cover. If Shiffon didn't have to kill her, she thought Harmony could've been an excellent candidate for Bad Bitches Only.

"Yes. Like I said, I would've done anything for him. Martina wanted to ruin Enzo if she couldn't have him for herself. I had no choice but to kill her."

"Turn it off." Alex pushed the phone away and stood up. He couldn't stand listening to anymore of it. "How do you know this woman is telling the truth and isn't just one of his obsessed fans?"

"She's obsessed alright but she's also telling the truth. Harmony gave us her phone and the passcode," Shiffon said, taking the phone out and handing it to Alex. He was reluctant to look because he knew if he did, he could no longer be in denial.

"I don't know what to say." Alex stood in front of the massive floor to ceiling window, staring out at the city's skyline view. "Enzo's stunt could've single handedly brought down Fortune Five Records. He was willing to jeopardize everything I built, so he could be on top. The crazy part is he actually pulled it off. He's one of the biggest artist in the world right now. Instead of Taz Boy leading with his own single, he had to settle with being a feature on Enzo's record." Alex let out a heavy sigh.

"I know this is a lot to process but you believed Taz Boy was set up and you were right. I guess that should give you some satisfaction."

"It should but it doesn't. Now I understand when I was growing up, what my mother meant when she would say, sometimes the truth ain't meant to be known, so don't go looking for it."

"I'm sorry. I know this isn't what you wanted to hear," Shiffon said, feeling guilty for being the one to bring him the bad news. She was used to seeing the intimidating, mean mug stare plastered across Alex's face but never this look of devastation.

"No need to say you're sorry. If anything I owe you

an apology, Shiffon. I gave you a hard time. Honestly, I doubted you. I had almost zero confidence you would get the job done. You proved me wrong and that rarely, if ever happens to me. Congratulations." Alex reached out to shake Shiffon's hand.

"Thank you." Shiffon blushed. "I'm not gonna lie, this was a tough one but we got it done."

"You never told me what happened to the woman in the video. You did handle it...right?" Alex wanted confirmation.

"Of course. You hired and paid me quite well to do a job. I take that very seriously. If you go look out your window. Harmony should be at the bottom of the East River. We tied her up with rope and weighed her down with a forty pound kettlebell on each leg."

"Very impressive. I'm sure I'll be utilizing your services again."

"I look forward to it."

"It should go without saying, that what you found out regarding Enzo, stays between Bad Bitches Only and me. No one else." Alex made that clear.

"Of course. Like I always say, strictly business. But I have to go. Another job awaits me. Bye, Alex."

"Not bye. More like until we meet again."

The two exchanged smiles and Shiffon walked out the door feeling on top of the world."

Epilogue

TWO MONTHS LATER...

Shiffon was pulling up in the parking lot, ready to go inside a very upscale but extremely private restaurant in the Chastain Park section of Atlanta, when a breaking news story caught her attention. She turned up her radio and listened intently.

R&B Superstar Enzo was found dead this afternoon in his hotel suite of an apparent accidental drug overdose. The singer was coming off a huge night after winning multiple Grammy's including best album last night at the award ceremony. Fans across the world are mourning the sudden death of the singer. His meteoric rise to fame...

Shiffon turned off her radio. She didn't need to hear anything else after that. "Accidental my ass!" She sighed slamming her car door shut. "I guess Alex handled Enzo in his own way."

She decided to put all thoughts of Alex, Enzo and Fortune Five Records out of her mind, wanting to stay mentally prepared for the potential new client she was meeting. Binky said the man was willing to pay a premium price if she was able to get the job done. With a growing business, Shiffon needed those checks to balloon too.

"You must be Shiffon," the rather tall man stood up and said when she got to his table.

"Yes, and you must be Faizon. It's a pleasure to meet you," she said, shaking his hand before taking her seat. "So how can I solve your problem?" Shiffon asked.

"I like you already. I've never had anyone pose a question to me in those terms."

"That is what you're hiring me for. To make a problem go away."

"Very true," Faizon agreed.

"So tell me what the problem is and hopefully I can get it resolved within your timeline."

"Beautiful and professional. I'm already convinced you'll be perfect for this job. I'm in the pharmaceutical business, in layman's terms a drug dealer. I move a lot of weight. But recently I've taken some major hits. And it's all because of one man, who they call King. I need you to kill him for me."

"Sounds simple enough but if that was the case, you wouldn't need to pay me an exorbitant amount of money to get it done."

"Here's the problem. That nigga move wit' so much silence, you might as well call him a ghost. It's probably why he keep on rising in the game and no one has been able to take him down."

"I see. I'm assuming King is his last name, do you have a first name to go with it?" Shiffon questioned.

"Fuck no," Faizon shook his head. "I don't even think King is his last name. It's just a title the streets gave him because he's been on top for so long. He's become the anointed King of these streets. But I'm counting on you to take him off his throne. Can you do it?"

"There's only one way to find out. Hire me for the job."

"I was sold the moment I saw you walking up to my table. It's yours."

"Then let's get started. We'll call this mission, Killing The King."

Coming Soon

A KING PRODUCTION
Bad Bitches Only
ASSASSINS...
EPISODE 3
(Killing The King)
JOY DEJA KING

A KING PRODUCTION
The Legacy
Keep The Family Close...
A Novel
JOY DEJA KING

Chapter One

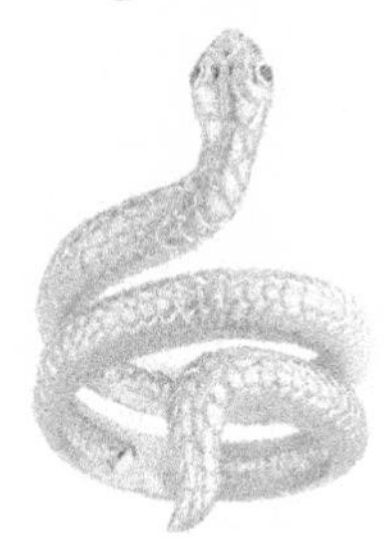

Raised By Wolves

"Alejo, we've been doing business for many years and my intention is for there to be many more. But I do have some concerns..."

"That's why we're meeting today," Alejo interjected, cutting Allen off. I've made you a very wealthy man. You've made millions and millions of dollars from my family..."

"And you've made that and much more from our family," Clayton snapped, this time being the one to cut Alejo off. "So let's acknowledge this being a mutual beneficial relationship between both of our families."

Alejo slit his eyes at Clayton, feeling disrespected, his anger rested upon him. Clayton was the youngest son of Allen Collins but also the most vocal. Alejo then turned towards his son Damacio who sat calmly not saying a word in his father's defense, which further enraged the dictator of the Hernandez family.

An ominous quietness engulfed the room as the Collins family remained seated on one side of the table and the Hernandez family occupied the other.

"I think we can agree that over the years we've created a successful business relationship that works for all parties involved," Kasir said, speaking up and trying to be the voice of reason and peacemaker for what was quickly turning into enemy territory. "No one wants to create new problems. We only want to fix the one we currently have so we can all move forward."

"Kasir, I've always liked you," Alejo said with a half smile. "You've continuously conducted yourself with class and respect. Others can learn a lot from you."

"Others, meaning your crooked ass nephews," Clayton barked not ignoring the jab Alejo was taking at him. He then pointed his finger at Felipe and Hector, making sure that everyone at the table knew exactly who he was speaking of since there were a dozen family members on the Hernandez side of the table.

Chaos quickly erupted within the Hernandez family as the members began having a heated exchange amongst each other. They were speaking Spanish and although neither Allen nor Clayton understood what was being said, Kasir spoke the language fluently.

"Dad, I think we need to fall back and not let this

meeting get any further out of control. Let's table this discussion for a later date," Kasir told his father in a very low tone.

"Fuck that! We ain't tabling shit. As much money as we bring to this fuckin' table and these snakes want to short us. Nah, I ain't having it. That shit ends today," Clayton stated, not backing down.

"You come here and insult me and my family with your outrageous accusations," Alejo stood up and yelled, pushing back the single silver curl that kept falling over his forehead. "I will not tolerate such insults from the likes of you. My family does good business. You clearly cannot say the same."

"This is what you call good business," Clayton shot back, placing his iPhone on the center of the table. Then pressing play on the video that was sent to him.

Alejo grabbed the phone from off the table and watched the video intently, scrutinizing every detail. After he was satisfied he then handed it to his son Damacio, who after viewing, passed it around to the other family members at the table.

"What's on that video?" Kasir questioned his brother.

"I want to know the same thing," his father stated.

"Let's just say that not only are those two motherfuckers stealing from us, they're stealing from they own fuckin' family too," Clayton huffed, leaning back in his chair, pleased that he had the proof to back up his claims.

"We owe your family an apology," Damacio said, as his father sat back down in his chair with a glaze of defeat in his eyes. It was obvious the old man hated to be wrong and had no intentions of admitting it, so his son had to do it for him.

"Does that mean my concerns will be addressed and handled properly?" Allen Collins questioned.

"Of course. You have my word that this matter will be corrected in the very near future and there is no need for you to worry, as it won't happen again. Please accept my apology on behalf of my entire family," Damacio said, reaching over to shake each of their hands.

"Thank you, Damacio," Allen said giving a firm handshake. "I'll be in touch soon."

"Of course. Business will resume as usual and we look forward to it," Damacio made clear before the men gathered their belongings and began to make their exit.

"Wait!" shouted Alejo. The Collins men stopped in their tracks and turned towards him.

"Father, what are you doing?" Damacio asked, confused by his sudden outburst.

"There is something that needs to be addressed and no one is leaving this room until it's done," Alejo demanded.

With smooth ease, Clayton rested his arm towards the back of his pants, placing his hand on the Glock 20–10mm auto. Before the meeting, the Collins' men had agreed to have their security team wait outside in the parking lot instead of coming in the building, so it wouldn't be a hostile environment. But that didn't stop Clayton from taking his own precautions. He eyed his brother Kasir who maintained his typical calm demeanor that annoyed the fuck out of Clayton.

"Alejo, what else needs to be said that wasn't already discussed?" Allen asked, showing no signs of distress.

"Please, come take a seat," Alejo said politely. Allen stared at Alejo then turned to his two sons and nodded his head as the three men walked back towards their chairs.

Alejo wasted no time and immediately began his over the top speech. "I was born in Mexico and raised by wolves. I was taught that you kill or be killed. When I rose to power by slaughtering my enemies and my friends, I felt no shame," Alejo stated, looking around at everyone sitting at the table. His son Damacio swallowed hard as his Adam's apple seemed to be throbbing out of his neck.

"As I got older and had my own family, I decided I didn't want that for my children. I wanted them to understand the importance of loyalty, honor, and respect," Alejo said proudly, speaking with his thick Spanish accent, which was heavier than usual. He moved away from his chair and began to pace the floor as he spoke. "Without understanding the meaning of being loyal, honoring, and respecting your family, you're worthless. Family forgives but some things are unforgivable so you have no place on this earth or in my family."

Then, without warning and before anyone had even noticed, blood was squirting from Felipe's slit throat. With the same precision and quickness, Alejo took his sharp pocketknife and slit Hector's throat too. Everyone was too stunned and taken aback to stutter a word.

Alejo wiped the blood off his pocketknife on the white shirt that a now dead Felipe was wearing. He kept wiping until the knife was clean. "That is what happens when you are disloyal. It will not be tolerated... ever." Alejo made direct contact with each of his family members at the round table before focusing on Allen. "I want to personally apologize to you and your sons. I do not condone what Felipe and Hector did and they have now paid the price with their lives."

"Apology accepted," Allen said.

"Yeah, now let's get the fuck outta here," Clayton whispered to his father as the three men stood in unison, not speaking another word until they were out the building.

"What type of shit was that?" Kasir mumbled.

"I told you that old man was fuckin' crazy," Clayton said shaking his head as they got into their waiting SUV.

"I think we all knew he was crazy just not that crazy. Alejo know he could've slit them boys' throats after we left," Allen huffed. "He just wanted us to see the fuckin' blood too and ruin our afternoon," he added before chuckling.

"I think it was more than just that," Clayton replied, looking out the tinted window as the driver pulled out the parking lot.

"Then what?" Kasir questioned.

"I think old man Alejo was trying to make a point, not only to his family members but to us too."

"You might be right, Clayton."

"I know I'm right. We need to keep all eyes on Alejo 'cause I don't trust him. He might've killed his crooked ass nephews to show good faith but trust me that man hates to ever be wrong about anything. What he did to his nephews is probably what he really wanted to do to us but he knew nobody would've left that building alive. The only truth Alejo spoke in there was he was raised by wolves," Clayton scoffed leaning back in the car seat.

All three men remained silent for the duration of the drive. Each pondering what had transpired in what was supposed to be a simple business meeting that turned into a double homicide. They also thought about the point Clayton said Alejo was trying to make. No one wanted that to be true as their business with the Hernandez family was a lucrative one for everyone involved. But for men like Alejo, sometimes pride held more value than the almighty dollar, which made him extremely dangerous.

A KING PRODUCTION
The Legacy
Part II
Keep The Family Close...
A Novel
JOY DEJA KING

P.O. Box 912
Collierville, TN 38027

A KING PRODUCTION

www.joydejaking.com
www.twitter.com/joydejaking

ORDER FORM

Name:

Address:

City/State:

Zip:

QUANTITY	TITLES	PRICE	TOTAL
	Bitch	$15.00	
	Bitch Reloaded	$15.00	
	The Bitch Is Back	$15.00	
	Queen Bitch	$15.00	
	Last Bitch Standing	$15.00	
	Superstar	$15.00	
	Ride Wit' Me	$12.00	
	Ride Wit' Me Part 2	$15.00	
	Stackin' Paper	$15.00	
	Trife Life To Lavish	$15.00	
	Trife Life To Lavish II	$15.00	
	Stackin' Paper II	$15.00	
	Rich or Famous	$15.00	
	Rich or Famous Part 2	$15.00	
	Rich or Famous Part 3	$15.00	
	Bitch A New Beginning	$15.00	
	Mafia Princess Part 1	$15.00	
	Mafia Princess Part 2	$15.00	
	Mafia Princess Part 3	$15.00	
	Mafia Princess Part 4	$15.00	
	Mafia Princess Part 5	$15.00	
	Boss Bitch	$15.00	
	Baller Bitches Vol. 1	$15.00	
	Baller Bitches Vol. 2	$15.00	
	Baller Bitches Vol. 3	$15.00	
	Bad Bitch	$15.00	
	Still The Baddest Bitch	$15.00	
	Power	$15.00	
	Power Part 2	$15.00	
	Drake	$15.00	
	Drake Part 2	$15.00	
	Female Hustler	$15.00	
	Female Hustler Part 2	$15.00	
	Female Hustler Part 3	$15.00	
	Female Hustler Part 4	$15.00	
	Female Hustler Part 5	$15.00	
	Female Hustler Part 6	$15.00	
	Princess Fever "Birthday Bash"	$6.00	
	Nico Carter The Men Of The Bitch Series	$15.00	
	Bitch The Beginning Of The End	$15.00	
	Supreme...Men Of The Bitch Series	$15.00	
	Bitch The Final Chapter	$15.00	
	Stackin' Paper III	$15.00	
	Men Of The Bitch Series And The Women Who Love Them	$15.00	
	Coke Like The 80s	$15.00	
	Baller Bitches The Reunion Vol. 4	$15.00	
	Stackin' Paper IV	$15.00	
	The Legacy	$15.00	
	Lovin' Thy Enemy	$15.00	
	Stackin' Paper V	$15.00	
	The Legacy Part 2	$15.00	
	Assassins - Episode 1	$11.00	
	Assassins - Episode 2	$11.00	
	Bitch Chronicles	$40.00	

Shipping/Handling (Via Priority Mail) $7.50 1-2 Books, $15.00 3-4 Books add $1.95 for ea. Additional book.
Total: $__________FORMS OF ACCEPTED PAYMENTS: Certified or government issued checks and money Orders, all mail in orders take 5-7 Business days to be delivered

CPSIA information can be obtained
at www.ICGtesting.com
Printed in the USA
LVHW111540190419
614848LV00001B/45/P

9 781942 217367